Ride A Cowboy

BWWM Romance Novel

JAMILA JASPER

Copyright © 2017 Jamila Jasper

www.jamilajasperromance.com

ISBN:9781521511947

DEDICATION

Dedicated to you, my readers.

JAMILA JASPER

CONTENTS

Acknowledgments   i

Prologue   1

1   Aja   29

2   Fatal Attraction   94

3   3 Months Later   148

4   The Robinsons'   206
Secret

5   The Search   271

6   Out For Blood   331

7   ...Will Be   391
Brought to the
Light

8   Happy After All   447

ACKNOWLEDGMENTS

A.H.V. You are my rock and the very reason I am where I am today. I love you more than you'll ever know.

PROLOGUE

The fog was rolling back over the road, and Steel Gray felt, in some strange way, the symbolism of the whole thing. These last few years he'd been in a fog of his own. The army had been his life for so long, and he had the scars- some physical, some internal- to show for it.

Now it would be different. He was opening a new chapter. As he held the wheel of his truck steady, he recalled the conversation he'd had with Carson Tucker, his cousin.

"You watch, Steel," Carson had chuckled. "Country life ain't all bad. Give it a month, you'll be singing a different tune."

Carson had given Steel the use of Tucker Ranch, an enormous piece of land in Boyd, Virginia, which Steel would be seeing for the first time in only a couple hours. He'd spend the next year there, perhaps longer, since Carson seemed to want nothing to do with Tucker Ranch or Boyd, Virginia, ever again.

"I just need to clear my head," he'd told Carson. His cousin had chuckled.

"Boyd's the perfect place. Nothing to think about, and shit-all to do."

He liked the sound of that.

At 9AM, he stopped at a rest stop in Denburg. The deeper he drove into Virginia, strip malls gave way to forests, and forests became rolling blue mountains capped with clouds of mist. He saw less towns with less people in them. The gas station was completely empty, like the fast food restaurants next to it.

"Ain't you a handsome one," said the aging station attendant. She eyed him approvingly. Steel was a large man, towering at six-foot five. Still in his early forties, His frame was densely packed with muscle; his hands were large and calloused. His height alone could intimidate, but his chiseled features, curly blonde hair and bright blue eyes made him striking to look at indeed.

"Where you from, honey?"

"New York."

She eyed him up and down. "Naw, where you *really* from?"

"Texas," he amended, amused.

She chuckled. "Now that's right. I see country all over you." She squinted. "Bet you don't scare easy. You in the force?"

"I was in the army," he confirmed, a little thrown by her assessment. Steel had grown up on a ranch in Texas, herding cattle with his Uncle Samuel until he was old enough to go to college. He had left the prairies of Texas and never looked back. "I know hard work. Is it my size?"

The attendant swiped his card. "Maybe. You've got a common look about you. I seen city folks, and they don't look like you."

That made him smile. "Thank you for your service," she called as he retreated to the car.

He was soon back on the road. He wasn't hungry, really. He didn't feel anything but a distant, fading ache. He forgot about the gas station lady and the beautiful blue mountains. He forgot about the last six months, the past disappearing as quickly as the miles disappeared under the wheels of his Toyota. That was his greatest talent, probably, Steel thought. Forgetting.

***

Boyd was exactly as he'd pictured it: small. Like a town frozen in time, with hand-painted storefront signs, wooden buildings, and a desolate feeling, all against a stunning backdrop of the Shenandoah mountains. The nearest port of civilization was forty-five minutes away- he'd counted.

Steel loved it.

What he didn't love, he soon discovered, were the outright stares. Some looks he got verged on hostile. They stared at his car, they stared at his New York license plate, and they stared at him, as he exited the truck and headed to the grocery store.

Carson had left Steel three instructions before they'd parted ways.

"Number one," he'd said, "The keys to the house are with Jerry. Old fella. Bald. Works at the grocery. Tell him I sent ya."

"Two, use anything in the house you want. Do what you want with it, just don't burn it down. Got it?"

Steel laughed. "Sure."

"Number three. Avoid the Robinsons."

Then Carson had changed the subject.

***

Steel found himself entering a quiet convenience store that doubled as the local grocery. The man behind the counter could have only been Jerry. Jerry was old, bald, and gruff. He didn't give Steel a warm country welcome; he seemed completely disinterested, in fact. But he handed Steel the keys, which were in a rusty tin on the counter, without a fuss.

"So you're Carson's kin."

"Yep."

"He owes me money," Jerry grumbled. His bottom lip was distended by the pouch of tobacco he'd plugged in there. Steel eyed another rusty can on the counter, this one filled with brown spit.

"Really."

"Yep. Wonder if he remembers that, while he's muckin' around in that bed of sin called California." Jerry looked at Steel accusingly.

"Sorry," said Steel, at a loss for how to respond. Jerry eyed him beadily all the way out of the store.

***

The road to Tucker Ranch was narrow and winding, but his truck made it easily. The Tucker House was a massive obstruction to the view of the mountains. Three stories tall, and almost as wide, it's design was grotesquely out of order with the modest wooden buildings he'd seen in Boyd.

As he pulled in closer, he noticed movement in front of it.

There was an old black man, sitting on a stump. The man had cloudy white hair, a liver-spotted face, and a bottle in his hand that he was scowling at intently. When Steel's truck pulled in he got to his feet.

"Hello," said Steel, climbing out of the truck. " Who are you?"

"Don't you worry about it, " snapped the man. For someone so small, he snapped power and authority with every word. He said nothing for a minute, surveying Steel's enormous frame, from the old leather boots to the curly gold hair.

"Hmmph. Ah already know who you are. You look just like 'em." He fell quiet again, his jaw working.

"Look like who? Who are you?" Steel demanded, his irritation mounting.

Before he could blink, the old man raised the bottle and smashed it hard against the stump. Glass flew everywhere. Liquor splashed on his shirt.

"You sure do look like them lyin' Tuckers," he said viciously.

Then he turned around abruptly and shuffled away, clenching the jagged neck of the bottle like a knife.

Stunned, Steel watched the man creep out of sight. He moved across the property towards an old fence that had once enclosed a horse pasture. Steel watched, mystified, as young black kid appeared and took the old geezer by the arm. They spared no glance for Steel. The two limped over the hill together and vanished.

***

Steel spent the rest of the week exploring the ranch, recollecting the days of his youth. There was a lot of work to do in the way of repairs. But luckily there were no animals to tend. He was a little disappointed, having entertained a romantic notion of himself riding astride a horse again. In no time he realized he was glad that the only living thing in this isolated wilderness was himself. The Tucker property was immense and lonely. That was good. He'd done enough worrying about other people to last him a whole lifetime.

So Steel worked. His city living hadn't purged his basic knowledge of how to fix things, how to hammer a nail, how to lay a board evenly. He'd always been a stubborn, do-it-yourself kind of guy, the value of hard work instilled in him from young by his old Uncle Samuel. Steel went to Jerry's once, to pick up food, which he prepared and ate himself. Then he got back to tinkering around the house.

The nightmares barely touched him that week. But when the sun went down on Monday, they came again.

He woke covered in sweat. He'd twisted around the blankets in his sleep. The light of dawn was peeping through his window. Of course. His body was still trapped in military time.

"Shit."

He went outside to meet the early morning. Dawn came clear and cold in the Shenandoah. Birds chorused in the trees. Spring flowers were opening under the cover of the dew, which would soon dry once the sun rose to meet the middle of the sky.

Steel noticed none of that. His mind was still on combat, thinking of torn uniforms, shouting, blood in the dust. It was always the same nightmare, but it always left him shaken. Not many things could shake Steel Gray.

He rolled his shoulders. Flexed his arms. Hell. He needed to relax. Only three things helped the nerves: a smoke, coffee, or a woman. He only had a cigarette.

And he discovered, as he lit it, that he also had a visitor.

"Hi," said the young black boy. Steel was always stunned by how soundlessly young children could move.

It was the same kid who had led the old man away a few days ago.

Like the old man, the kid was sitting on the old stump, where only yesterday Steel had cleaned up the broken glass from the old man's bottle. He was a small kid, skinny, with very neat cornrows, wearing a pair of old battered jeans and Nikes. He had dark skin and very large blue eyes. The contrast should have been unsettling, but it wasn't.

"This is the second time you've trespassed on my property," said Steel, more amused than irritated. Curiosity got the better of him. He took a seat on the stoop.

"Yeah? So?" said the kid.

"Was that old man your grandpa?"

"Yeah. Crazy Buck, they call him in town. But he ain't so bad."

"Why are you here?" said Steel.
He guiltily ashed his cigarette.
Couldn't smoke in front of a kid.

"I got a right to be here," said the
kid boldly.

"Oh? You know Carson?"

"Carson Tucker? Yeah I know
him. Y'all look alike."

Steel asked a question that had
been on his mind since meeting
the crazy old man with the bottle.

"Are you a Robinson?"

The kid looked surprised by the
question, as if Steel were an idiot
for asking.

"Uh, yeah. Drew Robinson."

Huh, thought Steel. Carson's warning rang in his ears, but it sounded ridiculous now. The insolent expression on this kid's face didn't seem particularly frightening. Steel Gray, military man, afraid of an old man and some kid?

"I got two brothers too," said Drew. "Daniel and Travis. And a sister."

He smiled impishly. "You was pretty jumped-up the other day. Didn't think a military man scared like that." .

"You got a smart mouth, huh?" said Steel. He found himself liking the kid. "How old are you?"

"Twelve."

Steel glanced at his watch. It was 7:30 AM. Shouldn't this brat be getting ready for school?

"Guess it's time you went home."

"You kicking me out?"

"Maybe. You wanna find out?"

They eyed each other. Steel got a tingling sensation in his gut. The kid looked so damn familiar. Yeah he'd seen him a week before...but up close... there was something else.

"You know," Steel added, when the kid didn't move, "I don't mind you coming by. There's a lot of space out here. I'm sure you and your...grandpa...are used to running around here. But I'm a private man. And I don't like surprises."

"You gonna call the Sheriff on me?"

Steel had to laugh. The thought of calling anyone over some harmless mouthy kid was absurd. But then again, who knew how this town operated?

 "Of course not."

"You met the Sheriff yet?"

"Nope," said Steel.

"He's a dickhead," pronounced Drew, seeming to relish the word. Steel raised his eyebrows, amused.
"A dickhead," he repeated.

"Aw, that's just what Travis says. Don't tell grandpa I was cussin', cus it's the truth. He won't leave my sister alone. An' he's always lookin' for trouble with me."

"Really?" asked Steel, interest piqued. One thing he knew for certain- kids could always sniff out a bully better than adults.

"Don't believe me? You'll see."

"Sure, I believe you," said Steel. "How old is your sister?"

Drew eyed him. "Twenty-eight."

"The Sheriff likes her?"

"Yeah, something like that." Drew waved his hands dismissively. "He's a creep. We're the only black folks in town, you know. He picks on us."

Steel nodded. There wasn't a note of dishonesty about this kid, he seemed to like telling it as it is.

"Well, if you ever need any help with him, I'll stick up for you."

Drew looked skeptical. "He's about your size. Maybe bigger, I dunno. He's got a gun."

A smile crept across Steel's lips. "Well, so have I. This is America, last I checked."

Drew gave Steel another appraisal, checking to see whether he was carrying the aforementioned gun. Steel was not. Drew looked disappointed.

"Okay, Mister."

"Mr. Gray. Steel Gray."

"Okay, Mr. Gray."

"Yep, that's a promise. And now, it's about time you walked on home and went to school."

Drew blinked. He hopped off the stump. "Well, bye."

"See ya."

The kid gave a mocking salute, and strolled back down the path.

Steel followed him a ways. He ducked under the fence of what had once been the horse pasture, and disappeared.

***

Steel took the rest of the day to go through the whole Tucker estate. It was huge.

The Tuckers owned enormous sprawls of land, and part of the mountainside too. The exact dimensions of their estate were framed in the living room, next to a hand-drawn map.

The house was labeled, as was the barn, the shed, and the stable. There was a little building to the West, which Steel had not known about, labeled "The Help". He found that curious, but not as curious as the multiple sketched portraits of six generations of Tuckers. They lined the hallway to the kitchen. Each portrait portrayed typical farm people. There were some women and some men. It went all the way up to the present day, ending with Carson Tucker.

Steel's people did not have portraits. This was not surprising. His relation to Carson was rather distant. Steel's branch of Tuckers had left Boyd in the early 1900's for life elsewhere. He guessed it had not been a popular decision.

Carson had reached out to Steel shortly after Steel left the military. Carson had inherited the ranch from his Aunt Fiona, as the last surviving male Tucker. It seemed the Tuckers had a habit of either dying young and suddenly or living to extreme old age.

Carson had dug through the family records, made a couple calls, and found Steel, the only other Tucker relative. They'd gotten along well, but they both wanted different things. Steel wanted to retire from the world, Carson wanted the opposite. A deal was struck- Steel could stay at the ranch while Carson tried his luck in L.A.

Steel moved through the house, feeling the weight of its secrets. The Tuckers were rich and old. All rich and old families had secrets- but what were they?

He poked through cupboards, pulled books from the shelves. He almost broke his neck on the rickety staircase in the south wing- another thing to add to the mounting list of repairs.

Before he called it quits, he came to a stuffy room that he could only guess had been Aunt Fiona's. It was pristinely decorated. A thick layer of dust blanketed everything. A large bible- as identified by flowery gold lettering- sat on the bedside table. Strangely, the bible was untouched by the dust. Someone could have placed it there that morning.

Steel Gray didn't get creeped out easily. He picked up the bible. When was the last time he'd been to church? Perhaps he should start going.

Several pages were bookmarked- by braided locks of hair wound with gold wire. Thick, russet, Tucker hair. Now that was creepy.

He flicked idly through the pages, stopping at one passage from the

Book of Job, which was underlined no less than three times:

"He discovereth deep things out of darkness, and bringeth out to light the shadow of death."

Steel wasn't sure if he believed that. He'd seen his fair share of injustice. Sometimes, the bad people won.

"Pessimist," he muttered to himself. He placed the bible back on the dusty table, and closed the door behind him.

Night came rapidly after that. In the army his whole day had been structured. It was constant pressure, performing in front of others. In the heat of Afghanistan he could have died at any moment. He had watched it happen to others- even his friends. Now, with total freedom and endless time on his hands, he felt like a curious child. Perhaps he felt a little foolish too. But so what? He could do whatever he wanted. He had the money, and the time.

And right now, he really wanted a drink. He wondered if this podunk town had good whiskey.

CHAPTER ONE

AJA

Aja Robinson worked at The Birdcage, a bar that sat on the fringe of Boyd county, far enough to appease the conservative city council, but convenient enough for truckers and farmers to stop on their lunch breaks. Boyd was a working town, make no mistake, and Aja Robinson was a working girl.

The truckers mostly ignored her. That suited Aja just fine. She didn't like them getting too friendly, and she always had to watch her mouth when they did. Aja couldn't afford to get fired.

That night there were no truckers, just the nightly regulars, salty old country men who still weren't comfortable with the idea of someone like Aja serving them drinks. Aja did her rounds, making sure everyone's glass was topped up. She kept an eye on the tabs.

She made banter with Cleaver, the chef. She texted her younger brother, Daniel, to make sure Gramps and the boys were doing okay at home. Mostly she watched football on the grainy bar tv, and eavesdropped. It was tough keeping herself entertained on the late shift, especially on a weeknight.

"Steel Gray?"

Again they were talking about the newcomer. Aja was already tired of hearing about him from her family, but she turned an ear to the conversation.

"So he's Carson's cousin? Carson Tucker?" said Billy, a grizzled electrician, busy carving his initials into the table with a pocketknife.

"That's right," said Steve. Steve was a Logan, from one of these old Boyd families that had been around just about as long as the Tuckers had. He did not like Carson Tucker, and really he couldn't see himself liking any kin of those Tucker snobs on the hill. He frowned into his Guinness.

"Must be from the mother's side. Never heard Fiona talk about no Grays from Texas," continued Billy.

"You seen 'im yet? Got the Tucker look about 'im," said Steve.

"Tuckers was always a funny bunch," Billy conceded. " 'Steel'. Now that's a name."

Aja went back to watching football. She'd heard enough about this mysterious stranger, and to be honest she was tired of it. Not that the local interest in him was anything unusual. Nothing ever happened in Boyd, so anything new naturally had to be gossiped about a hundred ways before the locals moved on to another subject.

But all of them agreed on one thing. The military man bore an uncanny resemblance to a certain Sheriff Joe.

This fact became immediately apparent to Aja when the bar doors swung open, and Steel Gray himself came striding up to the counter. He was in a good mood.

Aja couldn't help but stare. He was tall- very tall. Muscular. His hands, when he placed them on the countertop, dwarfed hers. Aja found herself craning her neck to look him the eye.

"Howdy," he said. Steel was surprised to see such a beauty working at a place like this. He wasn't always so caught off guard by women, but this was a definite exception.

"Well, hi," said Aja carefully. His manner surprised her. It wasn't the typical awkwardness of the local Boyd men, nor the arrogance of most strangers that saw her only as a potential bed wench.

"Do you have any whiskey?"

"Er- I'll start you a tab. Knob Creek?"

"Sure."

He didn't actually look like most Tuckers, though he had the size, and the hair. There was something in his face, a glint of something warmer than his name. He watched her with frank interest. It was a little intimidating.

She poured his whiskey over ice and set it down on the counter. He swallowed it all at once. Then he looked her over, a small smile playing over his lips. It wasn't a sly smile, or a wicked smile. Just a smile.

"So, Miss Robinson," said Steel. "Let's get to know each other."

***

Steel enjoyed the surprised look on the bartender's face. In fact, he enjoyed the very sight of her. She was short. Her skin was a delicious velvet brown. She wore her hair natural, kept up in a bun. And she was plump, just like Steel liked his women. When he'd said her name, her lips came together in a surprised, kissable bow.

"How do you know my name?"

"I met your brother, Drew."

Aja rolled her eyes. "I guess he told you all about me."

Steel raised his hands in surrender. "He just came by for a visit."

"I'm gonna wring his neck. I told him not to mess with that place."

"It was alright," Steel said. "I don't mind the kid."

"But some do," Aja muttered, beginning to turn away.

"Well, I still don't know your first name," Steel cut in. "I'm Steel Gray."

"I know who you are," the woman replicd. Hell, thought Steel. Even her eyes were bewitching. "Call me Aja."

Steel became aware that every ear in the bar was strained towards their conversation. He leaned in on his elbows. He felt content.

"Can I get another whiskey, Aja?"

She poured him another. He noticed that for all he was undressing her with his eyes, she was doing the same- she was just better at hiding it. She kept her tone light and easy.

"So, Steel Gray. Everyone is curious about you."

"Really? What for?"

"Military man. Newcomer, related to those scary Tuckers," teased Aja. "A lot of questions there."

"I'm an open book," Steel replied. He liked the way she spoke, with a little bit of attitude under that warm southern politeness.

"How are you related to the Tuckers?" She asked.

"Carson's my cousin."

"Alright. What brings you to Boyd? Of all places?"

"I like the quiet," said Steel simply. "That's all."

She smirked. "Well, we got plenty of that here."

"My turn," said Steel. "Can I buy you a drink?"

Aja shook her head. Damn it, she was looking up through her eyelashes. He couldn't tell a single thing from her expression. "Not on the clock, Steel Gray."

"Okay, so next question.What's a beautiful woman like you stuck in Boyd for?"

Aja did look out of place in the humble, greasy atmosphere of the Birdcage. She was wearing a modest black outfit that hugged her curves in all the right places. Her nails were immaculately done, her skin was smooth and deep sienna, and her eyes were wide, brown and alluring. Damn, thought Steel. She should be up on a stage somewhere. Or in his bed.

Aja smiled to herself. Steel wondered if he should dial it back. He was very aggressively hitting on her.

"Even beautiful women have responsibilities."

"What do you do for fun?"

"I guess whatever other people do 'round here. I take care of my brothers, my grandpa, I go to work. Can't really drive. No license, no car. Livin' is a full-time job."

He thought, or maybe imagined, a note of bitterness in her voice. Aja was a beautiful bird in a beautiful cage. But there was a fiery streak to her, Steel could tell.

"Is the old man a handful?"

"Sometimes," admitted Aja. "His mind comes and goes. He's got a good memory, when he can find it."

Steel glanced around the bar. The Birdcage was small, but cozy. There were a lot of pictures hanging on the walls: men holding fish, the local baseball team, the owners, that kind of thing.

Hunched-over men drinking in the corner. It all seemed vaguely familiar, and Steel guessed this kind of place existed all across America. He'd probably been in a hundred bars like this one, before the military, back in his wilder days. He wished he could remember if he'd felt the same way he did now- peaceful.

Voices raised in the corner. Steel turned to see an old, grizzled farmer stamping up to the bar. The man laid a heavy hand on Steel's shoulder.

"City boy. You play cards?"

Steel looked quizzically at Aja, who shrugged.

"Yeah, I do."

"We need an impartial eye. Come here."

Steel followed the man to the back table - and so did Aja- where four men were hunched over a game. A modest pile of money was heaped in the center.

"Aw," Aja sighed. "Y'all know I can't have you gambling in here."

"Wouldn't be a problem if Dean wasn't a damn cheat," snapped Billy. "We always play civilized. Like gentlemen. Don't bring no commonness to this table, Dean Murphy."

Dean, a mustachioed old cowboy with a matchstick firmly clamped between his teeth, and a confederate flag pin on his lapel, flushed. He was the Chief of Police in the neighboring county of Washitaw, and not used to having his honor questioned.
 "Call me a cheat again, Billy, I'll turn you loose."

"So you want me to watch?" Steel cut in, before Billy could respond. He felt a little irritated; he'd rather keep talking to Aja.

"That's right. Just one round. We're almost done."

"More drinks?" asked Aja.

"Bring 'em over, honey," said Dean, not looking up from the table.

Steel took a seat and watched the game. It was a basic Devil's Run setup, with two teams playing for the middle.

The men played. Steel watched, or pretended to. His eyes kept drifting to Aja. She bustled about the bar, cleaning up, tinkering. She couldn't concentrate on the TV anymore.

Aja got a text from Daniel, her oldest younger brother. Daniel was 17, and took charge of the younger boys when Aja wasn't around.

All good. Travis out with friends at Paul's. Gramp in bed.

Aja sighed in relief. She was glad Drew was home, at least. He always got up to trouble when Travis was around.

Her eyes moved over to Steel. The townspeople had been right. He did look a lot like Sheriff Joe. Steel's features were just a little softer than Joe's. His easy smile and curly gold hair did a lot to hide it, but the likeness was there.. Right down to the glacier-blue eyes.

Aja liked the look of him sitting there, laughing with the Boyd men. She guessed this was their way of testing to see if the newcomer could be part of their group. For all their distrust of strangers, these old geezers liked to be around young, capable men like Steel. He probably reminded them of their younger days, and made them feel old and wise.

The low tones of Willie Nelson drifted through the bar, relaxing everyone. Darkness gathered outside. Aja Robinson checked the time. Two more hours on her shift.

The men determined that Dean was not, in fact, cheating in cards. And Steel Gray found he was actually enjoying himself.

Aja watched him from behind the bar. He sure cut a handsome figure. He had a broad chest. Big hands, which he rested on his knees when he laughed. She found herself wondering- improperly- how it would feel to be stroked by Steel Gray's hands, to feel him pressing her into the bed...

"Why don't you buy us a drink, son," suggested Billy. His nose had turned a very bright red, but he was grinning.

Steve, Dean and Tim agreed. Steel laughed and ordered a couple pitchers. When Aja set them down he resisted the urge to pull her into his lap.

"Now, Steel," said Billy, a humorous glint in his eye. "You ever seen a tractor?"

"Of course," chuckled Steel.

"You ever ride a horse? What do city boys do for fun?"

"Drink and eat, same as you," replied Steel. His memories of being on horseback, soaring over the Texas prairie, were fond ones. He found he didn't like being called a "city boy", but there was something playful and friendly about these old men, so he let it pass.

"I went up to the city once," Steve Logan put in. He still did not trust Steel fully. But the man had bought them all drinks, which counted for something, and in this light he didn't look too much like a Tucker after all.

"You went to Charlotte," Dean accused. "That ain't no real city."

"I met an Indian gal there," Steve continued. "That was back in '68.

Her daddy didn't like me. Wanted her to marry another Indian."

Steel felt Aja's eyes on their little group. He caught her gaze from across the bar. She smiled.

Dean grunted and took the matchstick he'd been chewing out of his mouth. "Indians are funny creatures. Remember Lynette's kid?"

Tim and Billy laughed. "I sure do," said Billy. Tim did not- he had been too young.

Billy explained to Steel: "Charlie Murphy. His mama was Lynette Murphy."

"My aunt," added Dean Murphy.

Billy went on, " Lynette was Preacher Murphy's daughter, y'see. But little Charlie's daddy was some no-count Cherokee from North Carolina-"

"Cherokee? There ain't no Cherokee around here." Tim interjected.

"Didn't I just say he was from Carolina? Anyway, the whole thing was a big scandal for Preacher Murphy, on account of Lynette and the Indian"- Billy glanced at Aja, and finished quickly- "Not being married."

But Steel had caught the look, as well as Billy's hasty correction, and drew his own conclusion. Of course it would be a scandal in a town like Boyd for the preacher's daughter to get caught up with a man from another race. It seemed prejudice still ran deep in these parts.

"Not being married?" he repeated easily. "I guess that's looked down on around here."

"He was an Indian," Dean repeated, as if that hadn't been clear.

The men shrugged. Billy continued, "We have our ways. Tradition, you know? Anyway, that Charlie Murphy kid was never right. Ran wild half the damn time. Kept askin' everyone about his Pa, then kept runnin' off just like he did. Preacher tried to set Lynette up with someone, get the kid a man in his life. But no one wanted the poor girl."

"She wasn't so bad," muttered Steve Logan, almost too quiet for anyone to hear.

"Then why didn't you marry her?" chuckled Dean.

"Aw, I dunno," Steve hedged. The men laughed. Steve had been pretty young when Lynette was in her prime.

"No one wanted her," confirmed Billy. "It was the 60's. Things was different, folks was more close-minded."

"Aw, no one but John Tucker," corrected Dean. "Remember?"

"Oh, I remember," Steve said. "The old bastard."

"Now, now," said Billy. "That's our friend Steel's kin."

Steel shrugged, unsure how to respond. "Never knew the fella."

He didn't want Billy to stop the story. Luckily, Billy liked an audience.

"John Tucker was a character. The Sheriff, back then. Everyone was afraid of old John, especially his family. But the Tuckers was always sort of isolated up there on that land. No one knew what the hell was goin' on. You heard stories all the time. And there was some madness in that family, to be sure."

"So what happened with Charlie?" asked Steel, returning them to the point.

"Well," explained Billy, "The long and short of it was, John Tucker tried to get little Charlie Murphy out of the way. I mean, his Ma told everyone she was waitin' for that Cherokee to come back. She didn't want any other man to be a Pa to Charlie. So old John Tucker figured, hell, if the brat was out of the way, then sure thing Lynnette would come to her senses, which meant she'd fall right into his bed. And hopefully bear him another bastard. John liked to sow his oats, if you catch my drift."

"John was married," Steve said, recollecting. "To Lydia Tucker."

"That's right. A bitter old cow if there ever was one. But he had his heart set on poor old Lynette. She was a pretty young thing, give her that," said Billy. "And once a Tucker wants something, y'know, they have a way of getting it."

"John probably thought this one wouldn't be any different," Steve said darkly. "Rumor was he'd had half the wives in Boyd. Couldn't throw a stone without hitting a Tucker bastard."

"What happened?" Steel pressed. The men were avoiding a point, he could tell.

"They found Charlie Tucker dead," said Steve Logan flatly. "A slug in his head."

"Christ," said Steel. He glanced at Aja, to see if she was listening. She was, but he couldn't read her expression. She looked away from his stare.

The men nodded. "Suicide, they determined," Steve said. "I never knew a nine-year-old to kill himself."

"What happened to Lynette?" asked Steel.

"John Tucker misunderstood," Billy answered wryly. "He thought Lynette would come runnin' to his arms like a scairt little dove."

"She didn't," said Steel.

"No sir. The mornin' after they buried little Charlie, Lynette Murphy walked to the Tucker place, shot the knees out of John Tucker while he slept, and walked into the mountains. That was the last we saw of her. "

Steel raised his eyebrows. "Whew."

Steve Logan shook his head. "Had the prettiest red hair."

"They say she went to live with the Cherokees," Billy finished. "But I think she just died."

A silence hung over the table. Aja was looking down at a glass, brow furrowed.

"I take it the Tuckers aren't popular around here," said Steel finally.

"No sir," said Billy. "That family's got secrets, and we here in Boyd ain't too fond of those. But you're alright, son. And so is Carson, for all he's funny as a three-legged hen."

"Yep," chuckled Dean, picking a splinter from his teeth. He'd chewed the ends off six matches by now; they made a neat little pile in front of him.

Billy eyed Steel speculatively. "Seems like you don't know too much about the Tuckers."

Steel shook his head. "I don't like to pry." He'd heard hardly anything about his mother's childhood growing up in Boyd. She'd been a quiet woman, not one to live in the past.

"Ever wonder what happened to the Tucker bastards?" asked

Steve, bushy brows raised. He was warming up to Steel.

"What happened?"

Billy laughed. "They disappeared. Packed up and hit the road. Only a couple are left now, but they stay low. No sense bringing up the past. And we treat each other fine, here in Boyd. It's not like the old days."

Dean shook his head. His voice was almost bitter. "That's right."

"How long has John Tucker been dead?" wondered Steel.

"Oh, he lived forever," answered Dean. "Fatherin' kids left and right. Died around eighty-eight?"

"Naw, eighty-five," said Billy.

"Say," said Steve, raising his voice, "Aja, didn't your daddy work for old John?"

They all turned to look at Aja, who seemed startled. "No, " she said softly. "That was Grandpa Buck."

Billy shrugged, as if it was all the same to him.

Time crawled on. Soon it was nine-thirty. The bar closed at ten. The men talked for a little longer, but didn't start up a new game.

"Well," Billy said to Steel, placing both hands on the table-top and hoisting himself up. "Time to pack it in, boys."

Steel watched them leave, and turned to Aja. He figured he

should head back home, but he was reluctant to leave so soon. Steel wasn't sure he liked the idea of Aja Robinson going home at this late hour, alone.

"Do you need help cleaning up? " He asked.

Aja smiled. "No, I'm alright. "

Steel watched her move around the bar, straightening tables and chairs. She seemed to understand that he didn't want to leave, and didn't say anything when he resumed his seat at the bar. They held a companionable silence.

Aja swept, wiped the counters. Steel sat perched on the stool. It was strange, how deep this sudden attraction went. He was aware that he should probably leave- in a town this small, rumors travelled fast. Maybe Aja didn't want any trouble over her name and reputation…

"You going to wait here all night? " Aja laughed.

"No Ma'am," said Steel, smiling. "I just like looking at you."

Aja took her time locking up. "Then I guess you can walk me home."

The night was cool and clear. Steel had never seen so many stars, twinkling in their seats. It was very peaceful, and the air coming down from the mountains had a tint of pine.

The darkness made Aja's features even more prominent. He wondered what she was thinking.

Aja wasn't sure how she felt about this handsome, tall stranger that in the space of a few hours she had developed such a powerful attraction to. On one hand, he seemed like a good man. He wasn't from around Boyd, which was a huge plus- men around here knew too much, and talked too much, for her liking. On the other hand, was it worth getting involved with something that she wasn't sure could last? She had no intentions of settling down with anyone from Boyd. And besides, he was a Tucker…

"What are you thinking?" She asked Steel.

"How pretty you look right now,"
Said Steel. He wanted to bite his
tongue off as soon as the words
were out of his mouth.

She smiled. "Anything else?
Maybe that you want to take me
out for a drink?"

Steel was startled for a moment,
but then he grinned. Aja thought
his smile was dangerous; it did
dangerous things to her. "Sounds
good to me."

The walk up the street was
peaceful. Steel had parked a
ways off. Again they came back to
the fact that Aja couldn't drive;
Steel couldn't believe it. In New
York City, where he spent several
years of his young adult life,
hardly anyone knew how to drive.
But that was New York! Steel

couldn't imagine living in such a small, closed-off place like Boyd with no form of escape.

He wondered how innocent Aja truly was- though she spoke easily enough to him, Steel could tell that she wasn't completely comfortable around men. Did she go on dates? Were there any men in her life?

He was about to hedge his bets and ask, when flashing blue and red lights came streaking up the street, taking them by surprise. A white car pulled up in front of them, with "SHERIFF" in great blue letters plastered on the side. Steel looked at Aja, who looked nervous once she saw the car.

The door opened, and a tall, lanky man in uniform stepped out.

Steel's eye went immediately to the gun at his hip, a beautiful, shiny Colt .45. Not every run-of-the-mill police officer got one of those- they were expensive. He wore a cowboy hat, crisp blue shirt, and shiny black boots. A rabbit's foot dangled from a keyring in his belt loop. The streetlamp threw the man's features in sharp relief, and Steel was surprised to see that this could indeed have been his own brother. They had the same curly hair- though Steel's was blonde, and a little longer. The Sheriff's was chestnut. They had the same strong nose, and the same icy blue eyes. Steel knew that this had to be Sheriff Joe; and the fella had an attitude to match.

"Good evenin' ," said the Sheriff pleasantly, hooking his thumbs in his belt. "So it's Aja Robinson. And the new Tucker boy. Thank you for your service, Sir," he said to Steel, tipping his hat mockingly. Word had travelled fast throughout Boyd regarding Steel's previous profession.

"You're welcome," Steel said. He immediately decided that he did not like this man.

The Sheriff smiled, and turned to Steel's companion. "Aja, Aja, remember what we talked about the other day? About your responsibilities?"

Aja glared at him. "Yeah, I remember. Don't do this right now Joe. Please."

"Just reminding you what I said. If you can't do the job, we can find plenty of people who can do it for you." Joe smirked. He took a couple steps and opened the back of his car.

A tall black kid scrambled out. He was probably about fifteen. His hair was in dreads. He was followed immediately after by Drew Robinson. Both wore expressions of combined guilt and rage. Steel guessed that the older of the two must be Travis, the middle brother.

Aja gasped and pulled Drew close to her. "What the hell is going on?"

"Seems your, um, brothers took a little stroll on the Tucker property. Thought they'd get away with a little vandalism." He pointed his night-stick at Travis.

"Did they actually do anything?" challenged Aja.

The Sheriff's eyes flickered in annoyance. "Intent is still considered-"

"Are they under arrest?" Steel cut in, with obvious heat in his voice. He didn't like the man's tone. And he especially didn't like the way he had handled these young boys. He was a man drunk on power, that much was abundantly clear, and Steel hated nothing more.

"Stay out of this," The Sheriff snapped.

"This took place on my property, so it's absolutely my concern. No, I will not be pressing charges on these kids, so you can let them go. No need to terrorize young boys over nothing."

"It's okay," said Travis, trying to calm down Aja. "Drew went over there and I went to get him, like you told me to."

"I thought you were with your friends!" Aja cried. Concern had melted away; now she just looked livid.

"Those delinquents from over the county line?" Sheriff Joe sneered. "If I catch these brats around Boyd again, there'll be hell to pay."

"Why don't you leave us alone?" Aja snapped, rounding on him. "Haven't you done enough to me?"

"It's not my intent to cause you distress," said the Sheriff, suddenly soothing and plaintive. The switch was so immediate it was sickening.

"Let's go," Travis muttered. "I'm sick of this shit."

"You can leave now," Steel informed the Sheriff.

Sheriff Joe never lost his smile. "Of course. Aja, do a better job watching those boys. That old lunatic isn't going to do it. You don't want me to make a call to social services."

"Are you threatening me?" Aja took a step towards him, fists curled.

"Hang on," said Steel, stepping in front of her. "What were you doing at my property in the first place?"

The Sheriff blinked, then said in a condescending tone, "Making my rounds of course. It's my job to keep this county safe from *thugs*."

"You can make it safer by not targeting children," Steel snapped, authority crackling in his voice.

The thought of a man like this talking down to him made his blood boil. The sight of Aja's face, and little Drew's drawn expression, made him feel crazy.

Aja hung her head as Joe drove away. "God damn it," she muttered.

"Sis-" began Travis. Aja put up a hand. "Not now. Take Drew home, okay?"

"I can give them a ride," Steel offered.

"No," said Aja firmly. "Let them walk. It's not too far."

The two boys slunk off up the road. Aja took a deep breath as she watched them. She was obviously in distress. Steel watched as her features changed, as she carefully constructed a mask to hide her emotions. It was a talent he only knew women to possess; concealing the worst of themselves to put on a pleasant face for others.

"It's difficult, isn't it?" said Steel. He pulled out a cigarette. "Trying to hold it all together."

"Tell me about it," Aja muttered. She watched him light it. Aja didn't smoke, but almost everyone in Boyd did. She supposed it was a better habit than chewing tobacco, which everyone in Boyd also did. To her surprise, she found the way he pulled in the smoke, and the way it spread out from his mouth, the quick little breath he took to pull it deep into his lungs, almost appealing. In fact, there were a lot of things about this man that she found appealing, against her better judgement.

"Would you like one?" Steel offered.

"No thanks," she said.

"Do you mind if I do?"

"Go ahead, go ahead."

They continued their walk. "I guess I should have walked back with them," she said. "But I know Joe. He just likes to scare me some. He won't really do anything."

She sounded like she was trying to convince herself as much as Steel.

"You sure about that?"

She nodded. "Oh yes."

"He's a hopped-up bully," said Steel. "I bet he's not too popular around here."

Aja snorted. "That's where you're wrong. Joe's a favorite around here. Boyd likes to think he's some kind of hero. He protects the town from outsiders. He protects the town from itself. Or so they think."

"So he just picks on your family?" Steel was beginning to see a rather nasty side to this sleepy southern town.

"That's right," said Aja.

"Why don't you do something?"

Aja looked at him. "Seriously?"

"You can't let him go after your brothers like that. Today he's putting them in the back of the car. Tomorrow he's giving them beatings. Bullies always escalate."

"Well, if you know so much about it," Aja snapped. "Tell me what I should do? I hold down whatever job I can get in this town. I keep them fed and in school- as much as I can, anyway. I can't do it all, and no one's out to help me, as far as I can tell."

"You'd be better off finding work outside Boyd."

"I can't drive," Aja said helplessly. "Grampa used to take me out to Washitaw. But then his mind started going, and it wasn't safe for him behind a wheel. I'm trapped here."

Steel felt the distress radiating off her, though her voice never raised or lowered. She was so matter-of-fact about it all. In his own mind, he saw the solution present itself as clear as day.

"Well. I'm not doing much around here," he began. "I could drive you wherever you need to go. Hell, I could teach you how to drive."

Aja's eyes widened. She couldn't believe it. "Seriously?"

"Sure. You got a permit?"

Aja rifled through her pockets, pulling out a battered wallet. She flicked through it. "Aha!" she cried triumphantly, holding up the small white plastic ID. "I sure do."

Steel grinned. He slipped his arm around her waist, and to his surprise, she naturally drew in next to him. Her smell was intoxicating, like cocoa and brown sugar and vanilla. Maybe it was something she used in her hair?

"Tell you what," he said. "Your first lesson is tonight."

Aja had no idea where this man had come from, but she was sure glad she'd met him. The thought of driving at night made her only a little nervous, but she felt safe and protected with Steel Gray. It was a strange feeling.

"Will it be OK? Driving- in this dark?"

"Sure. We can chase down that Sheriff if you want," he laughed. "And to be honest, I'm a little drunk."

Aja grinned. "Naw, you ain't."

He laughed. "OK, maybe not. But still." He rested his hand just above the curve of her ass, stroking her lower back. It was so good to touch her, after watching her all night. She kept her arm modestly curled around his waist.

He wondered if it was too early to pull her into the shadow of the roadside, and taste those beautiful full lips too.

"You're trouble for me," Aja said finally, as they came upon the parking lot.

"Naw, I ain't," he said playfully, mimicking her country drawl. Truth be told, the whiskey, and the good conversation, had put him in a very good mood, and heated his blood just a little. It had been a long time since he'd had a woman.

The streetlamp in the parking lot flickered- it had been needing a new bulb for months, but things moved slow around here. Steel wondered about the Robinson brothers, walking home by themselves.

"I know you're thinking about my brothers," said Aja, watching him glance up the road. "But I promise they'll be alright."

"I know," Steel smiled. "You're a good sister."

***

Steel's truck was red, and large. It was exactly the kind some wealthier kids of Boyd would drive- the Quesenberrys and the Logans, those kinds of folk. And it looked new.

Aja was a little stressed from the incident with Travis and Drew, but that sort of thing had become so commonplace she could hardly work herself up over it. She'd become numb to Sheriff Joe's antics for her attention, and it was only worry over how these things would affect the boys themselves that kept her up at night. How was constantly being targeted and painted as "criminals" affecting their self-esteem? Joe paid almost no attention to the other kids around Boyd- just Aja's family. If it wasn't Drew, it was Travis. If it wasn't Travis, it was Drew. Occasionally it was the both of them. They hadn't grown up with the love of their parents, like Aja and Daniel had. She had to set an example for them.

The first time the Sheriff had pulled the boys up in front of her, Aja had been terrified. She had been younger then, so it was mostly Travis and Daniel getting into trouble- although Daniel had always been more interested in his books than following Travis's harebrained schemes. Drew was still a little kid then.

Aja loved her brothers fiercely.
And she worried about them all
the time.

Steel tossed her the keys and
climbed into the passenger's seat.
Aja smiled. She knew she'd have
a protector in Steel. Apart from
the fact that he obviously liked
her- a fact she still didn't know
how to deal with- he seemed like
a good man. The way he had
stood up to Joe- well, she'd never
seen anyone do that. It was
because he wasn't from around
here; no one in Boyd would have
dared.

Had to be a Tucker, she thought,
as he turned to her, grinning. His
dusty blonde curls swung into his
face. She resisted the urge to
yank one.

"Well? You gonna drive this thing or sit pretty the whole night?"

"Aw, hush," she laughed, and turned the keys.

Aja did know the basics of driving- but it had been, admittedly, a very long time.

They pulled onto a back road, at her request. She wanted to take her time with this. Who knew when Steel would be able to take her driving again? She started off at a slow crawl, but a few minutes later, picked up speed.

"Now, you wanna go slow," Steel warned. "If your friend is out lurking again."

"No one goes down these roads," Aja said. She rolled down the window and pressed on the gas pedal. Oh, it felt so good to drive. The wind beat against her brown cheeks and sent Steel's hair tumbling backward.

"Can I go faster?" she begged.

Steel raised his eyebrows, though he was tempted to let her. "You're too green for that. I've cheated death enough times."

Aja quickly realized she had no idea where she was going- the last time she'd used these roads was with Grampa Buck, several years ago. She voiced this to Steel, who said he didn't mind. They could always turn back, and he had a pretty good sense of direction.

"So how old are you?" Aja asked.

"Forty-two."

She almost choked. "You look young. For your age."

"Forty's young," he protested.

"Forty-two," she emphasized, laughing.

He smiled. "And you're not yet thirty."

Aja shook her head. "I feel eighty sometimes."

"Don't waste your youth," Steel said, suddenly serious. "It's all we have. And once it's gone…it's gone."

Aja nodded. "Sometimes we don't have a choice. I feel like I never had a childhood. I've always been caring for other people. I love my brothers to death. And old Grandpa. Don't get me wrong. I'd do anything for them. But you know…I wonder sometimes. What it would be like."

She shook her head. The drive was easy now, though she'd picked up a bit of speed. "Does that make me a bad person?"

Steel thought about it. "No, I don't think so."

"Tell me about yourself," she said finally. "You know enough about me."

Steel didn't quite enjoy sharing details about his private life. But Aja seemed as honest as they came, and, well, he liked her.

"Well, I grew up in Texas," he began. "Moved to New York when I was a teen. Joined the army pretty young, and was in and out of it. Divorced a couple times."

" 'A couple times'? " Aja said, stunned. Then jokingly, "What's wrong with you?"

Steel laughed. It was a raspy, deep laugh, and she liked it very much. "We've all been fools in love."

Aja nodded. Well, that was definitely true, she thought bitterly.

"What else?" she probed. "Why did you leave?"

Steel shrugged uncomfortably. "Issues with management."

"What does that mean?" Aja wanted to kick herself as soon as the words left her mouth. Typical country girl, she chided. Asking too many questions.

"It's classified," he said easily. "All I know, is that sucker had what was coming to him. He was a Major. I challenged his orders. We had a…disagreement, that turned physical. That's what the paperwork says, anyway."

"Hmmm," Aja responded. She changed the subject. "You got any kids?"

"Nope."

"Do you want any?"

She caught herself trying to picture what their babies would look like. Get it together, girl. You only just met him.

Steel touched her thigh lightly. "You're veering to the other side."

"Whoops." Aja corrected herself.

Steel didn't answer the question, and he didn't take his hand from her thigh. He made small circles with the rough tips of his fingers. He thought how nice it would be to have both plump thighs wrapped around his face; he wondered what she would taste like.

"Let's turn back," Steel suggested. "I think we're pretty lost."

"You drive," Aja said.

They switched places. As they drove he reached across the seat and put a hand on her knee. Her skin was warm through her jeans.

"I might want kids someday," Steel said, several minutes later. "But first I want the right woman."

Aja looked at the twinkling lights of Boyd below. They'd driven all the way up to the mountains.

CHAPTER TWO
FATAL ATTRACTION

Up came the sun. Aja woke up the next morning in a daze. She could hardly remember the night before; it came to her in a series of pictures and images. She'd talked so long with the handsome stranger from Texas. Sheriff Joe had taken the boys, but Steel Gray made him leave them alone, made him disappear in his car. And then she'd actually driven, for longer than she'd intended, all the way up the Shenandoah Road into the mountains until the twinkling lights of Boyd looked like stars in the valley below.

Aja hugged her pillow. She'd been so excited, and dizzy, that she'd fallen asleep without her silk bonnet. She eyed the line of hair products on her armoire. The half-open closet door. The pile of clothes on the floor. She took in everything she saw, and then tuned her ears to listen to the voices below. The house the Robinsons lived in was old, like every house in Boyd, but it carried sound as easily as a church. By listening she could tell that Daniel was home, and so was Travis, and Drew. Grandpa Buck was laughing at something.

Aja loved her family very much. Her little brothers were her life. Her Grandpa had practically raised her. Aja loved their little house too, which had been in the family for a couple generations.

But secretly, in that innermost part of herself, she knew that she had to leave Boyd-someday. She was a young black woman in an all-white town. What kind of life was that?

But more importantly, she had to face the fact that life in Boyd was harming her brothers. They were constantly being targeted. Just last month, Travis had got in a fight at school over some kid calling him the n-word. And it had been Travis that the school had suspended.

Aja's thoughts then turned to the subject she'd been avoiding: Steel Gray. In one night he'd established himself in her thoughts, and now, try as she might, he wasn't going away. She went over all their interactions in her mind. The way he could turn from serious to joking. The assertive, commanding way he spoke that made you feel like sitting up straight and listening. His easy, playful sense of humor that seemed so out of character for a man of his size.

"Self control," Aja whispered firmly to herself. Of course Steel Gray wasn't the first man she'd developed feelings for over the last ten years. But Aja had to be careful. The men in Boyd only saw her as a prize, an exotic chocolate trophy to put on the shelf and collect dust. Aja wanted someone to shine for. She wanted someone worthy. She wanted a real man.

A knock on her door woke her from her reverie. She sat up in the bed. What day was it? Saturday? Which meant her first shift at the grocers started at nine.

"Come in."

It was Drew. The boy looked sleepy. His cornrows were already fraying- Drew's hair was quite fine, like her father's had been. She reminded herself to touch them up later.

"Morning, Aja," said Drew.

"Hey, honey."

"You mad at me 'bout last night?"

Aja remembered that she was supposed to have scolded them

for trespassing on the Tucker property. Shoot.

"We'll talk about it later, okay?"

"Awright." Drew was a sensitive kid, but could be tough as nails. Aja knew she shouldn't play favorites, but...well. Drew was everybody's baby. She couldn't help feeling extra protective of him.

"I'm going to work soon," She said. "Daniel's staying home to watch Gramps."

"Okay."

"You better stay out of trouble, you hear me?" She said severely. "Stay home with Daniel. Leave Travis alone."

Travis wasn't a bad kid, but they egged each other on. And Travis had a temper and a smart mouth that, undoubtedly, had not helped their interaction with Joe Snell the night before. Better safe than sorry. She'd have to have a word with Travis, too.

"I'm gonna do your hair later, alright?" She told him.

"Awright."

Drew stayed in her bed while she showered and got dressed. She wrapped her long, natural hair in a bun-Aja rarely wore it loose around her shoulders because of the attention it got.

"Drew?" She said softly when she was ready to leave. He'd fallen asleep in her bed. His blue eyes flickered open at her voice.

"See you later, honey."

"Later, Aja."

A small hand reached for hers. She squeezed it.

In the kitchen, Travis was eating Cheerios- taking fistfuls straight from the box and stuffing it right in his mouth. Aja glared. "You and I need to talk later. Tonight."

"Awright," he said innocently.

"Mornin'," called Daniel, from his favorite seat on the porch. Every summer the boys moved an old couch on the porch, but only Daniel ever used it. He liked to sit outside while he studied. Daniel

was the tallest of them all. He
kept his hair in a tight fade when
he could get it cut- which was only
if he could make it to the county
over.

The last to greet her was Grandpa
Buck. He was standing by the
bottle tree, as usual, looking at his
collection. Bottles were stuck all
over the branches of the great
dead maple tree, bottles from
many years ago all the way up to
the present. Grandpa said it was
an old slave's tradition. The
bottles trapped evil spirits in them
at night, and when the sun came
up, they were purified and set
free. Grandpa Buck tipped his hat
to her, then went back to staring
at the bottles. The tree was so
large its branches scraped the
side of the house. Aja reminded

herself to have them cut
sometime, before the summer
was out.

She turned to the little path that
led out of the little plot of
Robinson land. The walk into
Boyd took twenty minutes. Aja got
started, thankful that the heat of
the day was a few hours away.

She looked back at the house
forlornly. She loved being around
her family. But lately it was getting
harder to find the time.With Daniel
applying to college, money was
tight. She'd rather he stayed
home and study than go to work
in Boyd, if she could help it. She
did wish she didn't have to work
so much. But family came first.

***

Steel was already up, and eager to start the day. In the shower his thoughts turned to Aja. Her beautiful skin. The feeling of her plump thighs, when he had squeezed them in the car last night. He wondered how such a plain town like this could hide a jewel like Aja.

Thoughts of her dusky brown skin, her soft, full figure and plump bottom danced through his head. He felt a growing hardness in his groin at the thought of her. What appealed to him the most was her innocence, how modest she was. He could tell she had only been with a few men. Or perhaps she was a virgin? Steel pictured himself as the first to enter her, the first to sample that sweet cream between her legs, plunge through her virginity and spill his seed all over her brown thighs.

"Self control," he told himself. For God's sake, he couldn't be chasing women in a town so small without some caution. He could only guess how sensitive the country folks were about things like that. And he wasn't a wild beast, though Aja Robinson certainly made him feel like one. He'd never felt so strong an urge to pull a woman over his lap and ravish her.

Getting his thoughts under control took effort, but he did it. He turned the water off, toweled, and got dressed. There was a lot of work to be done around the place today, Steel reminded himself.

For starters, that damn staircase in the Eastern wing had to be fixed. There was a lot of brown nasty water coming out of the pipes there, too. Carson had asked him to box up Aunt Fiona's things. But the best, most exciting part of all- Steel wanted to clean up the stables. It was his intention to buy a horse at some point.

He had eggs and toast and cold raspberry jam for breakfast. He sensed it would be a hot day. Nothing that he wasn't used to though. As he was washing up, he noticed movement out the kitchen window.

For a moment Steel thought he saw an old woman with white hair crossing his yard. But it was only the gathering sunlight, soft breeze, and the petals of the wild rosebushes climbing over the wooden fence.

A knock on the front door brought him out of it. It was little Drew Robinson. His hair was half picked-out, the black curls standing out from the remaining cornrows like a frizzy half-halo.

"Hey," said Drew. "G'morning."

"Hey," replied Steel. "You doing your hair?"

"Taking it out for Aja when she gets back," said Drew. He wore a bored, sleepy expression.

"She's not home?" asked Steel.

"Some people have to work for a living."

What a moody kid, Steel thought, amused. Then again, most twelve-year-olds were. "Did you eat?"

"Yeah," said Drew. "She does feed us, you know."

"Alright, smartass," Steel laughed. "What do you want?"

"Nothing. This house is kind of crappy, huh?" He pointed his chin at the fraying screen door, the bug-eaten doorframe. More and more repairs. Steel hadn't noticed half of that.

Steel snorted. "Alright, that's it. Home."

"Hey!" Drew yelped, as Steel cut around him and pushed him towards the path.

"Easy, kid," said Steel. "I'm coming with you."

"You wanna see our house? Why?"

"Well, I'm sick of you brats tumbling all over mine," said Steel lightly. "Besides, it's neighborly."

Steel didn't know what possessed him , but he felt a strong urge to see the Robinson place. Maybe it was better that Aja wasn't home. He could picture her not being very pleased with him surprising her suddenly. Well, call it curiosity. He wasn't the prying kind, but he'd take any avenue to get to know Aja Robinson a little better.

As they crossed a little pasture and started down the hill towards the Robinson house, Carson Tucker's warning rang in his ears.

"Look out for the Robinsons," his cousin had told him.

Why? Wondered Steel. They seemed harmless enough, apart from that crazy old man with the bottle. Maybe kind, friendly, Carson was just a racist. Jesus Christ.

Drew worked on more of his hair as they walked. His brown, quick fingers tugged harshly at the braids, then combed through the loose curls, picking apart the tangled ends.

"I came over to your place 'cus was bored," explained the kid. "Nothing ever happens over here."

"You didn't have enough excitement last night?" Steel wondered.

"Pshaw," said Drew, puffing his chest. "That wasn't nothing."

"Your sister was really worried. Why were you on Tucker property anyway?"

Drew looked defiant. "We been going over there for years. Even when Carson was livin' there."

"So?"

Drew scoffed. "We wasn't doin' nothing. Just walkin around."

Steel opened his mouth to reply, and Drew sighed. "Aw, don't. Already got my ear chewed off by Dan."

The big Texan laughed. "Well, then just remember what I said. Give me some warning, if you're hanging around there."

They came upon the Robinson place. Steel tried to hide his surprise. It was a small house, a little run-down. Wildflowers overran the garden- or what had once been the garden. A huge, dead maple tree stood to the left of the house. It's branches were covered with bottles of all colors and shapes and sizes. Grandpa Buck was sitting under it, smoking a pipe. Steel tensed, remembering their first encounter, but to his surprise the old man only smiled, and gave a friendly wave.

On the porch sat a young black kid who could have only been Daniel, the oldest Robinson brother. He looked very much like Aja, but the softness of her face gave way to harsh, stern angles on his. Daniel had a giant textbook open on his lap, a pile of flashcards sitting at his feet, and an old-fashioned pair of glasses on his nose.

He had wondered if Daniel would have blue eyes like Drew. He did not. His eyes were very large and very serious. They narrowed as Steel approached, intelligent and assessing over the wire rims of his glasses. Steel took one look at

Daniel Robinson and knew this was not a boy to be underestimated.

"Dan, this is Mr. Gray," said Drew.

"Hey there," said Steel, offering his hand.

"Hi," said Daniel. "So you stay at the Tucker place?"

"That's right," said Steel. "Drew took me over to say hi. Figured I'd be neighborly."

He looked around for Drew, but the boy had disappeared quietly inside the house, and Steel, feeling a little awkward, was left alone with Daniel. Daniel gestured to a chair, his tone friendly.

"So," said Daniel. "I guess you know all about the Tuckers?"

"Been hearing about them nonstop since I came here," Steel admitted. "Carson's a cousin of mine. But no, I don't know too much."

"I figured he'd fill you in if you was gonna stay in his house," said Daniel.

Steel cleared his throat. He had thought about that as well.

"So. What are you studying?"

Daniel hoisted up the textbook so Steel could read the title.

"Chemistry?"

"I want to be a doctor," said Daniel, with a slightly defensive edge to his voice. Steel wondered how often Daniel had had to defend his dream.

"That's great."

"Yup." Daniel shut the textbook. "So I heard you met Aja?"

Steel nodded.

"She's amazing," said Daniel.

Steel nodded again. He thought so too. "She thinks highly of you boys."

"I know," said Daniel. "We want the best for her. It's tough out here. I should work to help her, but she wants me to study."

He looked down at his textbook thoughtfully. "Without her I never would have made it this far in school."

"You're lucky to have her," Steel told him.

"B'lieve me, I know," said Daniel. "Do you come from a big family?"

"I was an only kid, so no," said Steel.

"An only kid. Is that why you joined the army?"

"What do you mean?" Steel wondered if everyone in this damn town knew his whole life story. Jesus.

Daniel tapped the cover of his textbook thoughtfully. "Looking for a brotherhood you never had. You know, I thought about joining. Hell, if I don't get into college, I think I might have to."

"I didn't join for that," said Steel. That's all he would say on the subject; no one had to know his reasoning. In truth he had enlisted because he was young and foolhardy, and the life had swept him away easily.

A breeze swayed the branches of the dead maple; the bottles clicked together in a ghostly chorus.

Little Drew came out of the house, sipping a can of iced tea. He took a seat on the steps. Daniel looked out at the yard thoughtfully. Grandpa Buck was still sitting under the tree. He looked so peaceful-perhaps he was sleeping.

"Did Aja tell you why Grandpa hates the Tuckers?" said Daniel suddenly.

Steel's eyebrows raised at this new turn of conversation. "No. She didn't."

"My grandma used to work for them, is what Gramps told me," said Daniel. "Since she was a little girl. There used to be more of our people in Boyd, back in the day."

He pushed the glasses up his nose. "They paid her next to nothin. Fed her scraps. Most days she wasn't allowed to leave the house."

"Christ," said Steel, disgusted. He could hardly believe these people were his own blood relatives.

"It was like slavery times back then," said Daniel. "No one knew what was goin' on."

"Right."

"Anyway, some people said Grandma had borne a Tucker bastard up there on the ranch, but if she did, no one knows what happened to it. I have my theories." He shook his head.

"How did she meet your granddad?"

"Back before he came to Boyd, Grandpa was a fighter in California - knife dueling, he told me. Ain't that wild? He came East

to get away from it, started workin'
as gardener for the Tuckers.He
was the gardener. They fell in love
and escaped. Came back to Boyd
after John Tucker died, with my
mom. Grandma died a year later.
We never met her. There was a
rumor that Ms. Fiona wanted to
leave our family something in the
will. A gift, to say sorry or
something. Ms. Fiona wasn't a
bad lady. She was really
Christian, y'see. She wanted to
clear her debts before she died."

"So what happened?"

"Don't know," Daniel said matter-
of-factly . "We never got a red
cent from the Tuckers. It was
probably just a story, anyway.
Probably not true."

Steel looked out at the peaceful old man. He wondered if that story was true, or just the delusions of an embittered old man, fed to his surviving grandchildren, which they believed because it was some sliver of hope that their situation could have a happy ending.

"Well," said Steel. He really had no idea what to say.

"I just want you to know, we don't blame you because you're a Tucker," said Daniel. "But there's bad blood there. And we got our reasons."

"I understand," said Steel. Daniel nodded, and went back to his Chemistry book.

***

At 2 o'clock that same day, Aja got off her shift at the grocer's. Her next shift started at seven. It was waitressing at Joe Blow's, which was clear across town- an hour walk, on a good day. She was just sitting and resting her legs outside Jerry's store when a familiar red pickup truck pulled into the parking lot.

Steel Gray leaned out the window. As usual, his curly blonde hair was tumbling all over his face, and his eyes were bright and mischievous. Aja had always thought military men were supposed to be serious. She remembered her Uncle Jack had been in the Navy. The few times she'd seen him, he'd never so much as smiled.

Now here came Steel Gray, with his shit-eating grin, his big hands slapping the side of his truck to some tune only he could hear.

 "You need a ride somewhere?" he called.

Aja was about to tell him no, she was fine, but something made her pause. It was her heart, skipping in her chest, and the sudden warmth spreading between her thighs at the sight of his strong, muscular frame stepping out of the truck to open the door for her.

"Alright," she said weakly.

His truck smelled like sage and rosemary. To her surprise there were big bushels of dried herbs in front of the passenger's seat, she had to open her legs to fit herself in. He didn't start the car yet, but leaned back, his hand resting on her headrest, watching her with those glacier-blue eyes.

"How are you, Miss Robinson?"

"Doing alright, and yourself?" she said politely. Every nerve in her body was humming at being so close to him.

"I'm alright. Was just up by your place. Came to say hi to the boys. Talked with Daniel a little."

"Oh, alright," she said. She racked her brains for something to add. Why did he make her feel this way- so nervous?

"You nervous?" he asked her, starting the car. She looked at him quickly. He wasn't laughing at her, or mocking. He just looked curious. Curious and hungry.

"Um, I need to go to Joe Blow's . It's across town."

He stared at her.

"It's just the name," Aja said, feeling an urge to giggle. "Don't look at me. I didn't come up with it."

Steel laughed. "Alright, Miss Aja. Miss Aja Robinson, working at Joe Blow's."

They drove across town.

"Your grandfather gave me these," said Steel, pointing his thumb at to the bundles of herbs between her feet. "Turns out he's got himself a little garden."

"Oh," said Aja. "The one out back? Mmm. They smell delicious."

Steel had Aja direct him across town. They parked in front of Joe Blow's. It was a small, pub-like looking restaurant, much like the bar where Steel and Aja had first met. Steel was surprised to see Aja break out in a huge, beautiful smile. She laughed to herself.

"You all right?" he asked.

"I can't believe Drew went over to your place this morning. He must really like you. He's usually so shy around strangers."

Steel shrugged. "He's a nice kid."

Aja nodded. "Yeah."

She made no move to get out of the truck. Steel noticed the way she pulled her full lower lip between her teeth, nibbling it in thought. He wanted to give it a nibble himself...

"You know," said Steel thoughtfully, reaching out to tug one of the kinky curls that sprung out the back of her scalp. "I've never seen you out of your uniform."

Aja shivered at his touch; his fingers reached to stroke the back of her neck, protectively, but with a firm authority she found both intimidating and irresistible. Steel turned sideways in his seat to look at her.

"You like it when I touch you?" His thumb stroked her full lower lip. His voice was soft and silken, like velvet. He moved his hand to cup the soft skin around her throat. Aja was plump, just like Steel liked his women, with a feminine roundness to her that drove him absolutely crazy.

"Yes," she whispered. "I like it."

Her big, beautiful brown eyes turned to his. Steel felt his heart jump. They were almond-shaped, with long dark lashes.

"When's your shift?" he asked, still speaking softly.

"Not for a while. At five."

He nodded. His hand dropped; he stroked the full curve of her breast

with the backs of his fingers,
circling her nipple through the
fabric of her shirt until it stiffened
and peaked under his touch.

"Do you want to go somewhere?"

She tore her gaze from his,
looking out into the parking lot.
Her breath hitched. "Yeah."

They didn't drive very long. Steel
had already risen and hardened
at the sight of her climbing into his
car; it took him everything he had
not to pull her over his lap and
have his way with her right there
in front of Blow's. *Patience*, he
told himself. It wouldn't do to lose
his composure and give the
townspeople any more reason to
talk.

They drove to a small pasture off the Shenandoah road, behind the curve of the small hill. Anyone walking along the dirt path could see them, but Steel didn't care.

"Kiss me," he commanded.

Aja blinked those luxurious lashes, her gaze searching. She leaned over and treated him to a generous view of her breasts, and the soft, teasing pull of her lips. He cupped her round face in his hands. God.

How did he want her? Turned over his knee, prying apart her pussy lips to sample her sweet cream with his fingers? On her knees, taking him in her mouth? Or turned around against the hood of the truck, that generous ass jiggling along the length of his cock? Their kiss deepened; Steel found that he didn't care how the hundred different fantasies he had played out in his mind would turn out in real life. All that mattered was Aja's panting as he worked the work shirt off her shoulders and unclasped the lacy white bra beneath; her full, brown-tipped breasts. They were generous and plump, with beautiful, perky nipples that he took immediately in his mouth as he pulled her over his lap. She buried her face in his neck as he suckled; he worked her skirt up.

"You smell amazing," he groaned through a mouthful of her breast. His fingers reached around to stroke the folds of her pussy through her lacy, tiny panties.

"Mmm," Aja whimpered. He was drawing wetness out of her, pushing her panties into the fold of her pussy, rubbing her clit through the cotton and lace. It was as if he simply enjoyed touching her, as if he wanted to get his own pleasure through making her squirm in ecstasy in his lap. Aja felt dwarfed by Steel. Even more so when he guided her hand to the hard bulge in his pants. She smothered a gasp. Even through the thick fabric of his denim she could tell he was a man of size.

His fingers delved into her pussy. He worked them in and out, drawing wetness all over her thighs. One arm clenched around her waist to keep her in place as his fingers fucked her; she writhed and moaned his name. "Oh, my god," she whimpered. She found herself pushing back on his fingers, wanting more inside her. She wanted to be filled with him, she wanted him to ravish her with more than his hands until she couldn't stand, until her pussy was flooded with his cum...

"Easy, babygirl," he whispered. "You'll get more. Soon."

Aja came hard, her whole body shaking, and he withdrew his fingers and pointed to the back seat.

"Take everything off."

She complied. He made no move to remove his own clothes. His gaze followed her hungrily as she doffed the bra completely, slid off the bunched-up skirt and lace panties, until she was completely naked in front of him. His gaze roved hungrily all over her. Hell, she was beautiful. Her eyes were dark with desire for him, but touched with a note of hesitation- she was still innocent, he realized. He would enjoy corrupting her, showing her how he wanted her to pleasure him- and then how to get pleasure for herself.

He got in back with her and spread open her legs.

"Touch your pussy," he instructed softly. "Touch it for me, Aja."

Aja began to rub her pussy, using the wetness of her first orgasm to stroke her clit.

"Do you touch your pussy? When you're in bed?" whispered Steel.

Aja shook her head. "N-no..not...uhhn..not really…"

"From now on you will. Every day. You're gonna touch it and think of me fucking you."

Aja moaned. Steel withdrew his cock from its constraints, placing it at the entrance to her moist love tunnel. He stroked it up and down, over her throbbing clit, coating the head with her juices.
Aja's eyes widened at his size. He was enormous.

"Uhn...wait.. You won't fit."

He shushed her. "Don't worry about that, baby. Keep playing

with your pussy until I tell you to stop."

Aja's fingers worked faster over her clit. Her dusky thighs trembled. She was mewling and whimpering, trying to angle herself to fit him inside her, even as she worried that he was too big to fit. He kept his dick firmly away. She wouldn't get the full pleasure his cock could give her until she made herself cum. There was nothing more Steel loved than a woman at the height of pleasure, and he loved to watch them fuck themselves to that point. He loved the way their faces looked, he loved their beautiful cries and moans. And Aja had never looked more beautiful.

"Put two fingers in your pussy," he ordered softly. She complied. He relished how submissive she was, and how the apprehension in her face gave way to a catlike, vulgar pleasure. He knew she would turn into a freak under his command, and he loved her even more for it. She worked the two fingers in and out of her pussy until they were coated in creamy juices.

"Taste yourself," he whispered. She put the fingers in her mouth and sucked the juices off them. Steel's imagination went wild. He wondered how good she would be at sucking his dick. Would she be able to take all of him down her throat at once? Or would she need practice- he wasn't a small man. Still, Aja was made of surprises.

Well, they had until 5 o' clock to find out. Cumming down Aja's throat appealed to him greatly, but he needed to feel her pussy first.

As Aja neared orgasm, Steel began to work the head of his cock inside her. She was tight as any virgin. He threw back his head and fought for control. The urge to fill her up with his cum was overwhelming, risk be damned. She was wet, wet and tight and hot. He felt her pussy drawing him in. Her pussy wanted her wedged on the full length of his dick, it wanted him to fuck into her tightness with abandon until he lost himself. He wanted the same thing.

Fuck it. Steel drove his full length into her all the way to the base.

Aja shrieked in pleasure; he began to pump in and out of her pussy rhythmically, enjoying the way her face contorted in sighs and squeals of pleasure. She was so beautiful, and right now she was his pretty, chocolate toy to use however he wanted… and Steel wanted her to feel good. He wanted her to cum on his dick again and again.

Their mingled pants and gasps steamed up the windows of the truck. Steel worked his cock in and out of her. He decided he wanted to see her on her knees. Ravishing her from behind was a fantasy he'd entertained since the moment he saw her generous ass twitching behind the bar as she hurried to make drinks.

"Turn around," he told her through his teeth. Just the sight of her pussy taking the full length of his dick was enough to make him throb so painfully it almost hurt.

"Yes," she moaned obediently. He had a thumb on her clit and rubbed it as he pumped into her. Her sizeable tits bounced and splayed over her chest from the percussion of his strokes. She made no move to turn until he withdrew his whole length from her pussy. She'd have to learn to listen.

" 'Yes, sir,'" he corrected.

"Yes, sir," Aja moaned. She turned over, presenting her ass and pussy to him. Her folds were slick with her desire. Running a finger inside her to see, he could tell how his cock had stretched her, and couldn't wait to do it again. He loved how she accepted his authority without question. She was so sweet and beautiful. He raised his hand and brought it down over her plump ass. She shrieked, but didn't move away.

"That's for not obeying me," he said. "Come here beautiful. Come get this dick."

Aja pushed back on his rigid member, her dark, beautiful ass trembling as she took in his size again. Steel clenched his teeth, willing himself to love her slowly. This position could be hard, when the woman could feel every inch of him inside her, stroking the secret places that danced the line between pleasure and pain...for

Aja, though, it was all pleasure. He loved the sight of her asshole puckering when he fucked her slow and deep. He loved the way her pussy clenched along his length, as if milking him for every drop he had. He picked up the pace.

"Oh...Oh my God," Aja cried.

"Touch your pussy again," he grunted. Her hands flew to her clit; she sobbed from fucking herself and from the pounding her pussy was taking from Steel's cock.

He squeezed her ass with both hands, smacked it, harder and harder, in time with his strokes. "Oh my god!" She screamed. "Yes, yes!"

"Yes who?" he demanded.

"Yes, sir!"

"Cum for me again." He plunged into her, deep and fast and rough, until her shrieks of pleasure filled his ears, until the frothy cream of her pussy coated his dick completely, until he could take it no longer, and jets of semen erupted from his balls and filled her completely. He pumped his seed into her womb until he was spent.

Aja was trembling in the throes of a final orgasm. She crumpled, his dick sliding out of her.

"God," he groaned. Steel was in a bit of shock himself. He had never lost control like that.

"Shoot," Aja muttered, feeling his cum slipping out of her womb. She wondered what day of her cycle she was on.

"I'm sorry," said Steel. "Didn't...didn't mean to lose control. Christ, Aja."

She had turned around to look at him, eyes wide and glowing. The effects of her pleasure were still apparent on her face.

"You alright?" He took her in his arms then, loving the way she felt completely naked against him. She was all woman, so feminine and soft. Her skin smelled like it had the other day- vanilla, brown sugar, cinnamon.

"Yeah," she whispered. "I haven't done that in a long time."

"It's okay, sweetheart," he told her, cupping her chin. "We can do it again, if you want."

She looked at him, eyes sparkling. "Don't you make me late for work."

Steel closed his eyes. What did he do to deserve such a woman?

"Well you can start," he said, feeling himself hardening again, "By cleaning up your mess. Use your mouth and tongue. No hands."

Aja bent to her task, but as if perfectly timed, her cellphone gave a cheerful ring.

She raised her head. "Shit."

Aja tried to conceal it, but Steel took a peek at the Caller ID before she dropped the call. It was Joe Snell.

"Why is he calling you?" He found himself asking sharply. Aja looked up, eyes narrowed.

"That's my business. "

The moment was over. He dropped her at Joe Blow's an hour early. She thanked him politely and walked away. Steel watched her as she did, his cock twitching. Damn it. What the hell was he getting himself into?

CHAPTER THREE

3 MONTHS LATER

Over the next three months, Steel Gray adjusted to life in Boyd. He found he had a knack for making things grow. The Tucker house was full of old gardening books, and there were plenty people in Boyd willing to give him seeds or cuttings. Under his care the garden became green and lush, with summer flowers pushing out buds that burst into color within the coming weeks, died, then budded again. He fixed up the house as much as possible. Boyd was full of repairmen that could come help him at a moment's notice. But Steel preferred to handle things himself, even what he wasn't sure about. It was a man's duty to make sure he knew how to do basic repairs in a home. He fixed the worm-eaten door frame, repaired the roof (which took ages, and eventually the help of Steve Logan to complete), and jimmy-rigged the plumbing so his showers stopped jumping from freezing cold to boiling hot. Mostly busy work.

For the hundredth time, Steel rejoiced and despaired that Boyd was such a simple place with hardly anything to do. Sometimes he missed the bustle of the city. He found himself thinking back on those days in the military- years ago, when he'd been stationed in places, like Seoul, like Los Angeles, that were bursting with life and energy. Yet now, he reflected, he welcomed the atmosphere of peace and quiet, which was occasionally disturbed by one of the Robinson brothers jumping the pasture fence to bug him.

The Robinson boys had decided that Steel was "cool people". They were on their summer vacation now. Daniel was busy studying as usual. Every weekend he headed to the public library to use the internet for his work.

Yesterday Dan had been sequestered in the upstairs office-what had once been John Tucker's study. His brothers preferred to be outside. When Travis couldn't find a ride to the next county to hang out with his school friends, he came to Steel's place with Drew. Of the three boys, Drew was the only constant. He'd taken a serious liking to the man from Texas, though it would kill his preteen ego to admit it.

Steel found the young boy following him everywhere. Drew was always at his elbow, helping him with repairs, handing him a tool he needed, or falling asleep on the porch while Steel went about his business outside the house. The boy was surprisingly handy. Whatever excuse got him out of the Robinson house and over the pasture fence, Drew made it.

For his part, Steel admitted that he'd taken a liking to the kid. He found himself adopting a fatherly tone when he spoke to him. Maybe that's what this whole thing was about, he reflected one evening. He was sitting on the porch watching Drew and Travis catch fireflies in an old tomato can. The kids just missed a father figure. In Drew's case, he missed something he'd never had.

The sun set over the edge of the mountains. Steel took a deep sip of his beer. He leaned his head back on the sofa, listening to the sounds of the forest and the great mountain that sheltered them. Like he'd done in the military a lifetime ago, he let his senses speak to him. The *waa-waa* of insects and the call of an owl...the laughs of Drew and his brother...

The setting sun splashed the whole yard- now a blooming garden- in orange and purple light. If he held still long enough, wildlife began to return to the scene. A pair of rabbits bounded towards their den. Deer skirted the edge of the property. He saw a robin return to its nest in the hollow of a maple tree.

Travis turned to him. "You did a real nice one with this place."

Steel smiled. Any compliment from Travis Robinson was rare, but always heartfelt.

The garden was indeed amazing. What a strange talent to find out about so late in life. He had a green thumb after all, a "call to the soil" as Daniel put it. But he couldn't have done it without the boys' help. Their company motivated him to finish things. He felt he had to be responsible.

His mind turned, as it usually did, to Aja.

Since that day in the Truck they'd been seeing each other more and more. He'd known it would be trouble to taste her a first time- and he'd been right. Now he couldn't get enough. She was like a drug, surging through veins, turning his head around.

Their meetings were frequent and intense. Often he found himself heading over to the Robinson place, where he could sit on the porch and talk to her all afternoon. Sometimes she made a big pitcher of lemonade. He learned that she was a damned good cook. One weekend she made a big lunch of fried chicken, greens, macaroni pie, mashed potatoes, sweet yams and cornbread with hot honey butter biscuits for dessert. She laid it all out on a big blanket in the yard. Steel and the boys put on their best, sat in the grass, and ate themselves sick. He'd stumbled back to his house and fallen asleep immediately.

Other times it was his turn to surprise her. Steel took her to the county over for a dance. They kicked their heels all night, Aja laughing in amazement at his rhythm, looking happy and flushed. He pulled her close to him, enjoying the generous curves of her body as much as he enjoyed her laughter and spunk.

They had sex all the time. And each time it got riskier.

Sometimes at work, on her breaks, he pulled her behind the building and hiked her skirt up, pressing her into the concrete wall from behind. She liked being fingered, he discovered. Sometimes the feeling of her cumming on his fingers wasn't enough; then he had to risk it all and make love to her for real. Her pussy was always as tight as the first time, no matter how wet she got, no matter how many times he plunged into it. But Aja was shy about doing it in public- she preferred to go back to his place, where he could press her into the deep bed and she could scream her pleasure to the hills and beyond.

They'd even done it in his truck again, right in front of the police station. That had been stupid, but she'd begged him to, and they'd come hard in each other's arms.

The other day he'd decided to introduce her mouth to his cock again. That time he wanted her to try deepthroating him. She started slowly. He was not a small man. But she was able to take a little of him at a time, and finally she got him all stuffed down her throat, and he was able to pump her wet sweet mouth easily. Soon he had her on her knees all the time- one of his favorite positions. It was easy to get her there- she seemed to love sucking dick, and after she'd done her job, he liked lifting her up and shooting another load in her juicy pussy for good measure. She took every drop. Some primal part of him liked knowing, as she straightened herself up to head back in public, that his thick cum was sitting inside her, leaking out of her fertile pussy all over her plump brown thighs, marking her as his. He wanted her to think about fucking him, day and night, the same way he thought about her. Still, he didn't know whether he liked cumming down her throat the best, or blasting his seed deep inside her.

But Aja was still a good girl, and he had to be careful. He didn't yet know her limits, though he was always testing them. She always seemed to surprise him.

The other day, as he was watching her juicy brown ass bounce along the length of his cock, he realized there was still another hole he hadn't tried. They were at the Tucker place, and it was dead quiet except for her moans. He wondered if he should go for it- would she like it? Did she think about getting her ass fucked- or had it never occurred to her? Knowing Aja, she would take it in for him- but he had to prepare her first.

He had decided to find out later. Aja was crying out- another orgasm- as he pumped in and out of her steamy wetness...

Something snapped him back to the present. He wasn't actually with Aja in bed, but watching the night unfold before him, sitting on the porch.

"Sick bastard," he muttered to himself. Thinking of that woman was a major distraction. He could lose himself in the very idea of her.

"Hey," said Drew, returning to the deck. The gathering darkness made his blue eyes glow like lamps. "Can I get some water?"

"Don't have to ask, kid."

Drew ducked inside. Travis took a seat on the step, looking at the firefly in the tomato can. Its light illuminated his dark face. He looked thoughtful. Then he tipped the can gently out onto the step, letting the little bug crawl away. It flexed its wings once- twice- then spiraled off into the darkness.

Out of the three Robinson brothers, Steel knew Travis gave the most trouble. He himself seldom was with Travis on his own, and he got the sense that Travis only came around because Drew wanted to. Travis adored his little brother, that much was clear. He was extremely protective of him. Perhaps he just didn't trust Steel.

He wasn't nice or polite- what you saw with Travis Robinson was what you got. He was real quiet, almost too quiet. But he had a streak of boldness- of authority- in him that never let anyone forget he was there.

Daniel came up the path as Drew emerged from the kitchen, clutching a pitcher of water.

"Ain't yall bored?" said Daniel.

"Nah," said Drew quickly. "I'm staying until Aja gets home."

Daniel shook his head. "Someone shoulda stayed behind with Gramps."

"Well, where were *you*?" said Travis.

"At the library. Working."

"I'm headed back," Daniel said, when no one answered him. Travis was staring off into the distance. Quiet again. Drew looked surly- he hated leaving, no matter how late it was.

Daniel eyed his brothers expectantly. "I ain't gonna clean that house myself."

When neither made a move, he kicked Travis' shoe.

"All right," snapped Travis.

The boys took only a minute to gather their things. Steel expected even Boyd kids to have video games and cellphones. The Robinson brothers didn't, or if they did, he'd never seen them use one.

"See ya, Mr. Gray." They trekked out, looking like three soldiers in single file down the path.

Steel waited a few more minutes on the porch. He'd had a pretty good day. The boys definitely gave the place some life. He liked talking to Daniel. He liked teaching Drew the basics of repair work. Today he'd even tried to teach the kid hand-to-hand fighting. Not the kind of stuff he'd picked up in the army, but the *real* messy stuff he picked up on the streets of Brooklyn in the 80's. *That* had interested Travis. The teenager hadn't say a word, but sat down and watched everything.

He definitely liked the boys, but it was Aja he thought about the most. He longed to see her more often. Lately he was realizing how much it would benefit the boys to have their sister around more during their vacation. The kids were always talking about her.

To tell it honest, Steel felt guilty for spending so much time with them when the one person they loved most in the world couldn't.

He decided it was time to give his cousin a call. He had some questions.

***

Steel lit a cigarette before he dialed. The phone rang for a solid minute before the drawl of Carson Tucker answered.

"Heya, cousin."

"Hi," said Steel. "How you doing?"

Since moving in, Steel hadn't heard much from his cousin in L.A. Not that he hadn't tried. The man was a devil to get ahold of.

"Pretty good, but I know that ain't why you called," Carson laughed. "Bored already up there?"

"Nope," said Steel, smiling. "There's plenty to keep me busy."

"Well, good. I don't know when I'll be back there, Steel, to tell you honest."

"I mean to tell you thanks," said Steel. "For letting me stay here. I do like it."

"What do you mean?" said Carson briskly. "Wasn't no trouble. The least I could do to thank you, for your service."

"Why not just sell it?" Steel suggested innocently.

"Look, I'm a modern man," Carson sighed. "But some things ought to stay within families."

It was an interesting comment, but not unusual, he supposed. He'd come to realize that Southerner's ties to the land ran deep, for sometimes the land was the only wealth they had. So Steel updated Carson on the repairs he'd done, and the people he'd met. He saved the subject of the Robinsons for last.

"I met the Robinson girl," Steel began cautiously. "Aja Robinson?"

"Oh?" said Carson.

"Yeah," said Steel. "They seem fine to me."

"Be careful, is all," said Carson. "I found that girl snoopin' around the property a few months ago. Twice. Second time I threatened to get the cops on her."

Steel was no stranger to Robinsons sneaking around the property. But Carson's tone surprised him.

"What was she doing?"

"Lord knows," Carson scoffed. "They're loose screws, is all. A lot of interestin' ideas. That old man especially. I 'member when the whole thing with the girl happened, when I caught her pokin' her nose about the yard. The next day he came runnin' at me screaming about some Will, some inheritance, he thinks they was owed by Aunt Fiona.

Apparently his wife used to work for Grandpa John?"

"Really," said Steel, recalling his conversation with Daniel.

"Yup. Now no one's askin' me, but I think the whole family's bad. They got a knack for gettin' in trouble. Especially the boys."

Steel felt a flame of irritation. He quelled it. *Play ignorant*. It wasn't time to argue with Carson Tucker. All he wanted was information.

"Hmm," he grunted.

Carson continued, "All I know is, I wouldn't trust that family. There was even rumors about the girl and Sheriff Joe. They're sneaky people, Steel. Jus' be careful."

"I will," said Steel. He struggled not to respond in kind to Carson's judgemental tone. "Now, I just had another question."

"Well, shoot."

"Do the Robinsons pay rent to you?"

"Nope," said Carson. "They got their own piece, like most everyone else in Boyd. Don't ask me how they paid for it, but it's theirs. I remember askin' Aunt Fee the same question, cus she was always talkin' about the land across the pasture, sayin' it was cursed. Apparently it nearly blew her down to find people wanted to live there."

"Cursed?" said Steel, startled.

Carson laughed. "You know us country folk, we believe in that sort of thing. Aunt Fee said she could hear ghosts howlin' there all night. She said it stopped when she sold it to the Robinsons."

"No kidding," Steel was caught between amusement and apprehension. He could hardly imagine why the Robinson land would be cursed. Perhaps another grisly story involving John Tucker? Now the only howling "ghosts" were just echoes from Grandpa Buck's tree bottles.

"Yup. She always had a soft spot for those people. Never did figure it out."

"Buck Robinson's wife was her nanny," Steel reminded him. "Maybe that was why."

"Oh, of course," said Carson. "Well, who knows?"

"Hmm."

"How did we even get on this subject?" laughed Carson. "I swear the mind gets away with me. Anyway Steel, you take care now. I appreciate you fixin' up the place. Send me a quote and I'll reimburse you."

"Oh, it's no trouble," said Steel quickly. Money was not a problem for him- and he'd enjoyed the work anyhow. "Did you want me to pack up Aunt Fiona's room?"

Carson exhaled heavily. "Don't bother if you don't feel like it," he said. "I know that place gives me the creeps. I'll hire someone to do it."

"Alright."

"Is that all, cuzzo?"

"Uhh, yeah. That's it."

"Alrighty. Buh-bye." Carson hung up.

Steel stared at his phone for a long time. He still had more questions, maybe more than he'd started with. But they'd have to wait. As the old Sergeant Burrows, Steel's mentor, had liked to say: *the two most powerful warriors are patience and time.*

Shit, he hadn't thought about the Sergeant in months. He'd been trying not to.

"No point to it," he said to himself. That was another thing. The more time he spent by himself, the more he talked to himself. The more he thought about the past.

He was about to go inside, but felt it would be a waste of the night. The house was far too big sometimes, and even Steel, who didn't believe in ghosts, had to admit it freaked him out a little, especially on these warm nights when the place settled in its foundations, groaning like an old man.

Instead, he stayed on the porch and thought of ideas for the garden. He'd put a street lamp in the middle of it. A vine, to crawl up and around the porch. A couple fruit trees.

But first, he wanted to do Aja's yard. Just a couple days ago she'd came through, admiring his work. She looked perfectly at home among the flowers, wearing a long, modest skirt, with her hair loose and bouncing freely around her shoulders. He wanted to take some baby's breath and place it in her kinky curls.

"We used to have flowers like this," he remembered Aja telling him as they admired his handiwork together. "When Mama was alive, you couldn't get her out of her garden if you tried. She learned from Grandpa."

"My dad had a garden, too," he told her, smiling at the memory.

She'd slipped her hand through his, gesturing to the blossoms. "I couldn't do this stuff. You're amazing."

"You're young," he'd laughed. "There's plenty of time to figure it out."

"And you're old," she teased. "But you got some other talents locked in there somewhere, I bet. You're suited to the country life. Next thing you know, you'll be startin' your own dairy farm."

Steel recollected his younger days on his Uncle's farm. How long had it been since he'd milked a cow? He fought back a smile.

***

Around 11 o' clock that night, a furious banging on the door woke Steel from his sleep.

Instinctively, he lurched to the door and flung it open- a careless move. He hadn't even armed himself. But when he saw his visitor, he relaxed immediately.

"To what do I owe the pleasure, Sheriff?" said Steel flatly. It took him a moment to realize the man was out of uniform. He wore a button-down shirt, jeans, and boots. A large, very serious looking blade was sheathed at his waist in a leather pouch.

"You can call me Joe when the badge isn't on," said Joe Snell, smirking. He peered around Steel's enormous frame, into the dimly lit hallway. "Did I rouse you from some peaceful sleep?"

"No," Steel lied. He made no move to invite the man in.

"Sorry about that. I ran a flat near the ranch. Figured I'd come up and talk to you proper. My first impression...perhaps wasn't that impressive."

Steel eyed the man. But damn, he was a tough snake to read. Snell's face betrayed no emotions. A small smirk played at the edge of his knife-thin lips. But his blue eyes were impassive. It was impossible to tell his game. Steel thought quickly. He still had some questions he'd like to pry from the Sheriff. This was the perfect chance.

"I don't mind sitting out for a minute," said Steel finally.

"Alrighty. Want a smoke?"

"Sure," said Steel. He took a seat on the porch sofa. Let the Sheriff sit on the step! Snell folded his long body into a squat. He took off his hat and scratched his head.

"This kind of thing is common in Boyd," Snell began. "Visiting your neighbor. They call it 'dropping in'."

"I've realized," said Steel. He thought of the Robinsons.

"Do you like it here?"

"Sure do," said Steel honestly. He needed to take control of this conversation, or he'd be the one answering questions all night. "Do you?"

Snell chuckled. "Of course. Ain't shit-all to do for a man like me. I like it peaceful."

"Nothing to do but catch vandals?" Steel said innocently. He took a long drag of the cigarette.
"I know what you think of me," Snell said. Through the haze of smoke, he hardly looked human, thought Steel. It was that expression. Every human had facial tics, ways of speaking that changed their expression. Emotions were fluid, and they reflected on the human face. But Joe Snell had mastered what few people ever could. His face was a mask. He betrayed nothing.

"And what's that?" said Steel.

"You think I pick on these boys. Truth is, I've got nothing but concern for them. Living in that crumbling house. You raise boys like these without a man in their life, they turn to criminal behavior. Trust me," he said, as if speaking to a halfwit or a child. "It happens all the time."

"I think Aja does just fine."

"Oh, Aja," said the Sheriff softly. Suddenly he looked sly. "You know her well?"

"A little," said Steel tightly.

"I'll tell you a little story about Aja Robinson," said Snell He ashed his cigarette and reached for another one. "I remember when she was a little hottentot. Back in the day, before Drew was born. She went to high school here in Boyd. Pretty young thing, and popular too."

Steel wished the man would stop talking. His face never changed expression, but his tone grew oily. "She had half the men in Boyd wrapped around her finger. I guess they wanted to be wrapped around her. In any way they could, if you catch my drift. And Aja thought she could play games."

"What are you getting at?" Steel demanded.

"Let me finish," the Sheriff held up his hand. "Thing about Aja was, she didn't know when to quit. Always forgetting her place-"

"Her place," Steel repeated. Disgust coiled in his gut. Did these people have any shame?

"Sure. We have rules in this town, same as anywhere," said Snell easily. "And when Fiona Tucker's brother- Carson's Uncle Pete, you may recall- started paying attention to little Aja, why, she just couldn't say no."

"She was a teenager," Steel said. "In high school."

"He was a married man," Joe shot back. "A lusty one, Pete Tucker. But women like Aja can't say no. It was the talk of the town. She was always after whatever hard cock she could get. And then Aja suddenly dropped out of school."

Steel felt his heart skip.

"At the same time Mrs. Robinson- she was still alive then- quit her job. And no one heard from the Robinsons for a year."

"Get to the point, Snell."

"Use your eyes," the Sheriff snapped, losing patience. "There's an odd one out in that family. It doesn't take a genius to see."

Steel knew. Truthfully, it had dawned on him a couple months ago. But there was something missing in this equation. Something wasn't adding up. He changed tactics.

"Why do you care?" he demanded. "It was years ago. Why are you telling me?"

Snell's eyebrows lowered. "I know you've been involved with the Robinsons. I know Aja has her own agenda on what happens with this property. There are rumors about Fiona Tucker's will, you know. That she meant to leave it all to the little black family next door. Some kind of get-me-to-heaven sacrifice. That old bat never wanted anything to do with the Tuckers, to tell it true. "

"I don't know what you're talking about."

"Let's not play dumb, between men," Snell said, smiling. "I know that you know. When there's no Will, the law divides all the remaining assets between the surviving Tucker relations. The legitimate ones, that is. Unfortunately Uncle Pete had an accident a short time before Fiona's heart attack. No one saw it coming."

"So what's your point?" demanded Steel. His tone was less than friendly.

"Oh, nothing. Just that Carson Tucker wouldn't be happy to hear that some uppity family was makin' schemes on his inheritance. He definitely wouldn't want to know that his own cousin, who he opened his home to, was helping them do it."

Steel looked at the man incredulously, trying to gauge whether he was being threatened.

"Anyway," continued Snell, taking advantage of Steel's silence. "I mean to ask you about Aja."

"Seems like that would be all my business," said Steel immediately. "And none of yours."

He was an inch away from kicking Snell off the property. It took all he had not to slam his fist into that greedy, smug face.

Snell ignored him, and said as if talking to himself, "She's beautiful still. Seems to have calmed down after her teens."

"What's your concern with her?"

"Should I be concerned? I've got no concerns, as long as she stays in her place. As long as you stay in yours. There's things about Aja Robinson you wouldn't understand. We have traditions here. Rules older than the both of us- and it's my job to see they're followed."

Steel recalled the mysterious calls Aja would get from this man, sometimes in the dead of the night. Calls she tried to hide from him. He remembered Drew saying that he targeted their family. And he realized, with a growing sense of disgust, that Sheriff Joe Snell was actually jealous.

"Stay the hell away from her."

"Aha," said Snell triumphantly. "You're fucking her, aren't you?"

"Get out." Steel stood up, and so did the Sheriff. His expression was inhuman.

"She sucks your cock good, doesn't she? You ever wonder who taught her that? Do you think about who might have owned that pussy before you?"

Steel moved towards him, but Joe backed away. Like all snakes, he made a good retreat. "Easy, big fella," Snell crowed, putting a hand on his waistband. "I'm armed. You're not. Don't make this easier for me."

"If you ever set foot on this property, I will kill you," Steel promised. His voice shook with rage. "And I won't need a gun to do it."

"Good talking to you," called Joe Snell mockingly. He sauntered down the path, whistling.

***

He couldn't sleep. That was the trouble- every time he shut his eyes he saw her face. Finally, he shrugged on a T-shirt and went outside. The screen door slammed behind him. He had to see her, touch her. Claim her again.

He crossed the pasture barefoot, dew wetting the bottoms of his jeans. The Robinson house loomed, pathetically small. All the windows were dark. But by some miracle, when he cut around Steel saw a figure sitting on the step. It was Aja. She had her head in her hands.

Steel could hardly believe it was her. He felt his head swimming at the sight of her.

"Aja," he called lowly.

She raised her head. "Steel? Is that you?"

"Yeah."

She peered into the darkness. "I don't see you, honey."

Was she afraid to come to him?

"Come to me. I'm here."

Aja was barefoot. She only wore a short, silky nightie. In the darkness she could see Steel's tall frame. A giant in the daylight, he looked almost frighteningly huge tonight. But it was Steel. The man who weeded her garden. The man she taught how to fish, the man who taught her how to shoot, the man who took her for wild, crazy rides up the mountain in his truck, who watched her little brothers, took her fishing and shooting, taught her how to defend herself. The man who wasn't afraid of anything.

She crept up to him, the nightie rubbing against her nipples. She wore nothing underneath it. In the low light she could make out his expression- impassive, almost cold. He looked angry. His curly gold hair caught the moonlight and made a blue halo around his head. His eyes were dark.

Steel wrapped her in his arms. She shuddered under his touch.

He was so much stronger than she; if he wanted he could break her in half. Yet as always he was gentle, firm but gentle.

"What's the matter?" Aja whispered. His silence was scaring her.

"You're alright?" he asked, his voice muffled by her hair.

"Yeah, I'm alright."

He drew back, hands on her shoulders. "The Sheriff came by the house tonight," he told her. Aja drew a breath. She thought carefully about what to say, but Steel's next words shattered her composure.

"Are you involved with him?"

Aja tore herself from his grasp. She looked for a sign in his eyes that he was joking, lying- and saw nothing. He looked extremely serious.

"Because if you are, Aja, I swear-"

"How dare you!" She almost shrieked. "Is this what this is about?"

She could hardly believe he'd just said something so horrible. This was Steel. Steel! The man she trusted. Horrified, she felt tears spring to her eyes. His own face remained remote. She could tell he still didn't believe her.

"Screw you," she choked. It took her all she had to keep from slapping him. She turned to walk away, back to the house, back to her room-

Steel wouldn't let her go. He followed her and pulled her back against him forcefully.

"Tell me. Make me believe it. What's going on with you two?"

Aja beat against his chest, but he wouldn't let her go.

"I don't owe you anything. Let me go, Steel."

"Are you?" he said.

"No!" she almost shouted. "I'm not. Never...never in a million years."

Still holding her to him, he felt the way she trembled. He heard the catch in her voice. She had to be telling the truth. "Tell me everything."

Aja felt the tears coming thick and fast, soaking into the fabric of Steel's cotton shirt. She had always hated people seeing her cry. She didn't want to be weak. "I can't," she said.

Steel shushed her. "It's alright," he said. "I'm here. Nothing is going to happen to you."

Slowly, Aja calmed down. When she spoke, her voice was steady and calm.

"I can't talk about it," she said. "It hurts too much. Please, Steel."

"I trust you," he said, and he realized that he did- he really and truly did. "It's alright. It's alright."

They stood like that for a long time. Steel worked out a lump in his throat. Aja opened her mouth three times, tempted to tell him everything about Joe Snell and what he had done to her- how he had ruined her life, how he had turned her away from men. But she was too afraid. What would Steel think of her? He'd lived in New York- she knew they had different ideas up there about women. Maybe it would make him more liberal. Maybe he'd understand. But when it came down to it, Aja was just too scared. And she hated herself for it.

Steel stroked her hair, cupped the back of her neck protectively. He could feel the slow thumping of her heart against his chest. *Damn it, Aja*, he thought. *I wish you would just tell me.*

"Come," he told her. "Let's walk."

"It's cold," she whispered, hesitating.

"Bring a blanket," he replied. "I'll warm you up."

She ducked back in the house and emerged with a thick acrylic throw. Steel wrapped it around her shoulders. Then they walked.

In the middle of the pasture that separated their properties, Steel took the blanket from Aja and laid it down. Then he lifted her up- she gave a surprised gasp- and laid her out in the middle of it. In the darkness her eyes looked big as silver dollars. She stared up at him until he knelt in front of her and drew the bottom of her slip over her creamy dark thighs.

Steel could see she was already wet. She was wet for him. He ducked his head to the secret place inside her, tongued her until he unlocked the moisture within her. He tasted and sipped and lapped at her until she trembled and cried out. Then he pushed two fingers inside, pumping them in her pussy, loving the feeling of her squirming in his palms, taking herself to the brink. Her clit stood out; he suckled it rhythmically. Aja's moans turned to gasps, her gasps to cries, which he muffled with a firm hand around her throat. She came explosively against him in a rush of juices. He drank them all greedily... and leaned up to kiss her so she could taste herself.

Aja glowed after each orgasm, but he wasn't finished with her yet. "Ride me," he commanded softly. He kicked off his jeans. Obedient as always, Aja lifted her slip and settled her wetness over his surging cock.

"It won't fit," she whispered. She could only take in the tip of him. Tonight he felt impossibly huge, and her pussy impossibly tight.

"Guide it in, baby," he instructed. "It will fit. You'll make it fit for me."

Mewling in pleasure, she slowly lowered herself over him. When she had him all the way, she gasped. She felt him filling her completely, stretching her pussy to accept his girth. He wanted her to feel every inch of him.

"Look at it," he told her. She did, slowly raising herself to ride him. "Uhnn.. Steel…"

"Watch me take you," he said. He pulled her flat against his chest and began to pump in an out of her with agonizing slowness. Aja buried her face in his mass of golden hair, against his neck. He smelled like pine needles, and grass, and manhood. She felt protected in his arms. She belonged to him, and he belonged to her.

"This is how I want you," he grunted into her ear, pummeling her harder. "Bent over. Taking me. Taking my seed…"

One arm held her fast to him while his left hand fisted in her hair, bringing her ear close to his mouth so he could whisper his plans for her and kiss her. That was the thing about Aja, Steel reflected, drowning in the heaven of her pussy, the melting softness of her lips. He could try being gentle. But she always brought a roughness out of him. He wanted to fuck her roughly, he wanted to make her cum again and again on his cock, and then he wanted to hold her in his big arms and be utterly tender.

"I'm cumming," Aja gasped. He rolled over and pinned her under him, the blanket tangling with their bodies. He was cold all over except where they were joined. He fucked her savagely. He made love to her sweetly, slow and hard. She cried his name and bit his shoulder, and at last he unloaded his seed into her, hot and creamy. It spilled out when he withdrew. She whimpered at the sudden feeling of emptiness. She'd still wanted more from him. It was never enough with Steel. He made her feel greedy. He made her feel alive.

Steel looked down at Aja's face, his head clearing from the fog of pleasure that overwhelmed them. That was the problem. He never knew where the hell he stood with her. She made him feel six things at once.

He cupped her face in his hands.

"Aja," he said.

"Yes," she replied. She was still catching her breath.

"You're mine. All of you."

"Okay."

"Say it for me."

"I'm yours," she whispered.

"As long as I'm here, I protect you."

They got up. Steel brushed the grass from her hair. The blanket was damp with dew, so Steel let Aja wear his shirt over her slip. He returned to the Tucker place bare-chested.

Then he lay in bed alone until dawn crept over the mountains.

CHAPTER FOUR

THE ROBINSON'S SECRET

It was Fourth of July weekend in Boyd. Folks were coming all the way from Wilminac County in the North to see the fireworks. For a week the little Shenandoah town had been preparing. The Fourth-July committee decided to host the yearly picnic on the lawn of Bethlehem Church. The potluck was organized through the church, but everyone in town would be going, and Steel was informed he would be expected.

"You're a newcomer and all," said Steve Logan, who had formed a sort of friendship with the Texas man. "But we're countin' on you to come by anyways and eat your fill. Just remember to bring somethin', you know. We all pull our weight for these things, even the fellas."

The morning of July Fourth came. Steel was of two minds on whether to go or not. He'd woken up that morning to Drew knocking on the screen door.

"Mr. Gray," called Drew. "You up yet?"

"Come in," Steel called from inside. He was on a stepladder trying to stuff a leak in the roof.

"Aw, I can't. Shoes is all muddy."

It had poured through the whole night. The yard was a swamp, and so cold Drew's breath was frosting in the air. He was in a hoodie and jeans.

Steel poked his shaggy head out the door. "Hey- Jesus God, it's cold," Steel swore. "Take off your shoes, kid. Come in."

They made eggs and bacon for breakfast. The kid sat at the table, flipping through a book of watercolors Steel had found the night before.

"Mr. Gray, you need a haircut," Drew observed.

Steel ran a finger through his tangled blonde mane. He grinned. "Maybe I ought to get cornrows."

Drew smiled, tugging one of his braids. "You goin' to the picnic today?"

Stirring his coffee, he eyed the gloomy weather. "Doesn't look too friendly out there."

"Yeah," said Drew. "We never went before. But Aja was talkin 'bout goin', this year."

"What do y'all do instead?"

Drew shrugged. "Grandpa used to barbecue. We stay home, mostly."

Steel looked at him. He wondered how much of the Robinson's seclusion was self-imposed, or perpetrated by the people of Boyd. Drew seemed very matter-of-fact about the whole thing.

Steel was curious. "Do y'all go to church?" he asked.

Drew shook his head. "We used to, back when Gramps could drive and we had the car. Over the county line, in Washitaw, they got a Baptist church we liked. The ladies was always real nice to us."

"Do they do anything for the Fourth?"

Drew looked suspiciously at Steel. "Yeah, I guess so. We went one year, when I was little."

Steel nodded. The shape of a plan began to form in his mind.

"Why?" asked Drew. "You ain't thinking 'bout missing the picnic?"

"Let's talk to your sister," said Steel.

***

Aja told Steel she'd already made plans to go to the picnic in Boyd. She laughed at his suggestion that they go over to Washitaw.

"I ain't seen these ladies in years," she snorted. "I can't just invite myself."

Steel watched her pace around her room. The sun was out, and things were clearing up. It seemed the picnic would go on after all- it just might be a little damp.

 Aja seemed more cheerful than usual, . She did her makeup in the little bathroom mirror. Steel watched her.

"You sure you wanna go to this thing?" he asked. There was a hint of nervousness behind her bright mood. She kept dropping things, picking slowly through her jewelry box, frowning at her reflection. Steel knew Aja Robinson well enough by now to tell when she was hiding something.

She put down her brushes. "Yeah. I'm on the fence about it."

"Why?"

Aja threw herself into the bed next to him with a sigh. He grinned and pulled her under him, straddling her waist with his hips. Aja shrieked and giggled; He buried his nose in her neck and gripped her waist.

"Why?" he asked, mouth on her throat.

"Mmmm. You know I can't think when you do that."

Steel smiled. Aja smelled like vanilla and almonds and brown sugar. She was warm and soft in his arms.

"So you don't want to go?" he asked.

"Nah," she said. "Maybe later, when the fun starts."

"Let's skip it," he said. "Let's skip the picnic."

"Oh yeah?" she laughed. "And do what? Stay here?"

"I'll take you riding."

"Riding?" Aja said, puzzled. "You mean riding horses?"

"Yup."

These last few months, in his never-ending free time, Steel had gotten back into riding, with the help of Steve Logan. He was a ways away from how he'd been in his youth. But in a sense it was like riding a bicycle- and Steel had always had a way with horses. Sometimes he found them to be as complex as people.

"You've been on a horse before, right?" he asked Aja.

She nodded. The idea of a day away from the bustle of Boyd- if Boyd ever "bustled" - was appealing.

"What will the boys do?"

"Well, whatever they want," Steel said. "Dan's old enough. So's Travis. I reckon they can figure out if they want to go to the Church, or stay at home, or do anything else. And Drew can tag along with 'em, or come with us."

"It's the Fourth of July," said Aja thoughtfully. "Independence."
"Yeah," said Steel, unsure where she was going.

"I guess we ought to let everyone be independent to choose what they want to do," Aja laughed. "Do you mind drivin' the boys somewhere, if they ask?"

Steel smiled. "No. You're gonna drive today. You need the practice. But sure."

She squeezed him. "So we'll go riding."

 "What about your Grandpa?"

Aja smiled. "He always stays home on the Fourth."

"Really?"

"Yep."

"Convenient," said Steel. He wondered about the old man sometimes. "You sure he's alright?"

Aja's brow creased. "Some days he's better than others."

***

Drew, Daniel and Travis went to the picnic. Or said they were going to, anyway. Daniel looked resigned when Aja asked him to watch his brothers.

The boys refused a ride from Steel. Aja and Steel watched them head on down the path. Aja wore a lilac blouse, tight blue jeans, and high cowboy boots. Purple suited her skin beautifully, Steel thought.

"You think they'll stay together?"

"I doubt it," Aja laughed. "But I gave them all some money, and at least Drew won't be alone. Daniel will watch him."

"Let's call them when we get back," Steel suggested. "You all should have dinner together. I know you don't get much time with 'em."

Aja beamed at the thought. "I sure will."

Her phone vibrated. Steel felt it through her pockets- he'd had a firm grip on her ass as he watched the boys walk away. If he was honest with himself, he'd much prefer to spend the day playing with Aja upstairs in her soft four-poster bed, finding new ways to make her cum.

"Shit," Aja muttered, pulling out her phone. She hastily ended the call, before he could see the ID.

"Let me run inside," she said suddenly. "I think I forgot something."

She began to pull away from him, but he held her fast. "It's Joe, isn't it? Don't lie to me, Aja."

She hung her head. "I have to call him back."

"Why? He threatening you?"

Her eyes went wide at the suggestion. Steel knew he'd hit a mark, and his blood was instantly up. That bastard. "Aja, so help me God-"

"Please! Just wait here."

She ducked inside. Steel felt his mood immediately sour. He breathed and calmed himself down. It didn't mean anything. She'd give him answers later- he'd demand answers from her. But for now, he wanted to enjoy his day.

"Hurts, doesn't it?" said a voice by his shoulder. Steel jumped. It was Grandpa Buck. He wore a brown jacket, yellow shirt, and faded blue jeans over a heavy pair of hiking boots. He had an unlit pipe in one hand, a bouquet of flowers in another. He smelled a little like spiced rum, but stood up straight as an arrow, and his voice was clear.

"What hurts?" said Steel carefully. Since their exchange on his first day in Boyd, he'd hardly said a word to the old man. Not without trying- Steel was a frequent visitor to the Robinson property, and and he made an effort to be polite. But Buck simply wasn't interested.

"Ah like you," said Buck, avoiding the question. He gave Steel a sharp look. "You seem like a good man. Ah can trust you with my granddaughter."

"Thank you... sir," said Steel. He couldn't have been more surprised than if the man had declared he'd won the lottery. He briefly reflected that Grandpa Buck was roughly the same age his father would have been.

As if reading his mind, Buck said, conversationally, "Who were your parents, boy?"

"Jane Tucker. She was uh, Fiona's little cousin. And Francis Gray was my Pa."

"Jane Tucker, huh? Never met that one."

Steel didn't answer. He could see
Buck trying to work something out
in his mind. The old man's mouth
opened and closed. It was hard to
believe that this man had been
one of the deadliest knife-fighters
in the country- if Daniel was to be
believed. Steel had a hard time
picturing it.

"Hm," he said finally. "Ah guess
Ah should tell you something.
Ain't really my secret to tell,
though..."

"Aja should be out soon," said
Steel quickly. He'd had enough
secrets to last him a lifetime. He
sure as hell wasn't itching for
more.

"Listen-" Grandpa Buck patted
his coat pockets frantically.

"Damn. You got a cigarette, Mr. Gray?"

Steel handed him one- he always kept an extra pack. He gave the man a light, and lit one for himself, too.

"Alright. Ah know Aja's gonna come out soon, so Ah'll make it quick."

"Alright," said Steel, resigned.

"Mind her talkin' to that no-good police fella? Joe Snell?"

Steel scowled.

"Yep. Now lemme ask you this. You notice sum'n funny about that one? Y'all bear a resemblance, you know."

"Yes," Steel said. Almost everyone in Boyd had remarked on the striking similarities between him and Joe Snell. Personally, Steel couldn't see it. The man was tall, but the likeness stopped there, he thought.

"He's a Tucker too," said Grandpa Buck, his dark eyes sparkling with hatred. "One of John Tucker's bastards."

"Christ Almighty," Steel swore.

"That ain't all," said the old man quickly. "Seems that bad Tucker blood runs strong. They can't keep the Rooster down, those Tuckers. Stick their cocks into anything. And they came after my grandbaby when she was hardly a woman."

"You mean Aja?" said Steel.

The old man looked urgently at Steel. "There's two things you gotta know, Mr. Gray. One, we got a Tucker in our very own family. You prob'ly guessed which one."

"I don't understand," said Steel. Though of course he did- it had to be Drew. The blue-eyed black child. The odd one out.

"Aja's mother and a Tucker-?"

"No, you fool," said Grandpa Buck, rapping Steel on the head, sprinkling ash all over his hair. "Aja. Little Drew ain't her brother. That's her son. Her own son. The son that Joe Snell- or maybe that bastard Pete Tucker- made on her. She was fifteen years old. Christ have Mercy. Only fifteen. "

Steel stared. Maybe he'd known all along. Maybe he'd been denying it. He remembered Joe's words vividly…

"Which one was it. Who did it?" he said huskily. He found it hard to see straight. His right hand clenched into a fist. Poor Aja. That poor kid.

"They both got her," Buck said, grabbing Steel's arm. "One night. They trapped her. She thought she was goin' to see Joe..She thought..." The old man's eyes blurred suddenly with tears. "Ah don't' know," he said finally. "Maybe it don't matter. It was all in the past, anyhow."

"Fucking hell."

"My daughter passed the chile off as hers. She didn't want Aja to bear the shame."

Steel heard Aja coming down the stairs. "Quick," he said to Grandpa Buck. "What was the second thing?"

Buck nodded, throwing a look at the door. "Fiona heard about what they did. She couldn't take it anymore- her family's sins." His eyes clouded; he was struggling to remember something important. Steel fought for patience.

"*She* told me-in the will- Fiona hid a second one- in the house-"

"What did they do with it?" Steel said urgently. "Who was responsible?"

"No one," Buck said. "It was never found. They never found nothin'. It all went to her only livin' relative-Carson. Your own cousin."

"Grandpa? Is that you?" Aja called from inside the house.

"Fiona had a diary," said Buck quickly. "In the house. She tol' Fiona had wrote it all down. Wrote down all of what she done, to be safe. Find the diary, find the will. Maybe them no-good Tuckers done right by us after all."

It sounded like Buck was talking about two different people, but it was too late for Steel to ask him. Aja emerged.

"Grandpa?" Aja said, smiling. "What you doin' out here?"

"Ah'm talkin' to Mr. Gray, sugar-mine," said Grandpa Buck. His voice snapped back to it's usual placid tone. He opened his arms to hug Aja when she came outside. Steel noticed her eye makeup was gone. Had she been crying?

"Where y'all goin' today?" he asked her kindly. His tone was so natural, but Steel was reeling from their conversation still. He found it hard to control his emotions- rage, rage and fire. He wanted to hit something. Especially at the sight of Aja's face. She had composed it, carefully arranging her expression. She was hiding her emotions. She was hiding it all from him- trying to be brave.

"We're going riding," Aja said, forcing a bright smile.

"Aw, horses? Well. Well y'all have fun."

"Yep. We might go to Mister Logan's. See you later, Gramps."

"Be good, sugar."

They walked to Steel's car. Steel's hands were shoved deep in his pockets. Clenched. Thunder clouded his brow. Aja, on her part, was totally silent. Guilty. Of course Steel knew that she hadn't really forgotten something in the house. He probably thought she was lying. He probably thought she was a whore- she was playing games-

They climbed into the truck- Steel held the door open for her.

"Aja," he said, once they were both inside.

She looked out the window, avoiding his gaze.

"Aja, look at me."

When she didn't, he cupped her chin and pulled her face to look him. This time she raised her gaze. It was half defiant, half guilty.

"What?" she whispered.

"It was him, wasn't it?"

She shook her head. "No, it wasn't."

Why did she keep lying? Why was she trying to protect Joe Snell? After what he'd done to her? For what purpose?

"You're lying to me."

"Yes," she said. "Okay? It was Joe. What can I do? He's got me. He's got me."

"What do you mean?" Steel said. He released her chin, leaning back in his seat. "You're a free woman. He can't control you."

"You can't protect me from everything!" Aja snapped. She hated how *good* he was! Steel, with the concerned blue eyes. With the soldier's touch. The brave heart that could do anything, stand up to anyone.

"I can protect you from him. Where is he? Right now? Take me to him."

"No."

"Damn it, Aja!" He slammed the steering wheel so hard she jumped.

"I owe him money," she said loudly. The harsh tone in her voice surprised her. "A lot of money. When Gramps got sick...a year ago. He needed surgery. And we didn't have insurance."

Steel let her continue. She took a deep breath.

"He said he'd help me. He had it- but it wasn't his money. I didn't know that. He just handed me the cash- and I thought I was doing the right thing. But then a couple months ago, before you came…" she took a deep breath. "He started asking for...favors, instead of payments. He wanted me to repay him in other ways. Otherwise, he said he'd frame me for stealing from Carson Tucker, and have Social Services on me. I'd lose the boys, the house..."

"Favors? What kind of *favors*?"

She clenched her fists. "You know exactly what kind."

"Jesus," Steel swore, looking at the roof of his truck. "Jesus Christ. Please tell me you said no. Tell me you didn't let him-"

"I didn't!" Aja cried indignantly. "After what he did to me- those years ago- I couldn't. I told him go to hell. But I need the money. He owes people too, and I need to come up with it."

"No. No you don't."

Aja took a deep, steady breath. Her next words sounded rehearsed, as if she'd repeated them to herself a hundred times before. "Daniel needs to go to college. The boys need money for school. I have to put food on the table. I have to save up for driving lessons. I have to pay that man back. I can do it."

"I have the money," Steel said. "I'll give it all to you. Right now. "

She shook her head. Her hands made fists on her lap again. Steel felt his pressure rising. He'd never felt such a confusing mix of emotions. Mostly rage. He hadn't been this angry in a very long time.

"Let me help you."

"I can't take your help. I can't owe anybody anymore."

"You're going to take this money. I have plenty of it. That's final, alright?"

"What you gonna want in return?" Aja snapped. There was a storm in her eyes. "No one is gonna own me like that anymore. I won't be in debt anymore."

"You don't have a choice, Aja!"

She tried to slap him; he caught her wrist. He wanted to turn her over his knee. He wanted to kiss her, make her see reason. Even at the height of her fury, she was so beautiful he could hardly stand it.

But the look on her face said she might claw his eyes out if he tried.

"Fine," he said shortly. He released her wrist.

"I'm leaving," Aja said. She opened the truck door. "Get off my property."

He said nothing. She stormed back to the house. He watched her slam the screen door. Grandpa Buck was still sitting on the porch, staring off into the distance, still as a stone. But Steel knew the old man had been watching.

Suddenly sick of Boyd, of the Robinsons, and of everything, he decided not to follow her. Steel turned the key in the engine and drove off. The fury was in him, choking him. He let it consume him. He didn't know where he was going, but his body knew what to do.

He drove straight to the picnic. He parked on the grass. He got out of the car.

People were milling about, dressed in their Sunday best. The smell of barbecuing meat and fried chicken drifted on the air- it was still early in the morning, but Boyd liked to do things punctually.

Steel walked through the small crowd, hardly noticing anything.

His mind was fixed to one purpose.

He was going to find Joe Snell. And he was going to kill him.

***

As fate would have it, Joe Snell was not at the picnic. Steel saw the Robinson boys in the distance. He realized that in some distant way, he was related to Drew Robinson. The boy was his own kin- no wonder he'd felt such a connection with him. The thought soured when he remembered Drew's origins. But the poor kid couldn't help who his Pa was. He couldn't help the circumstances of his birth any more than Steel could.

The more Steel searched, the more his anger cooled from

blazing fury to a slowly simmering rage. It wasn't just that an injustice had been done to Aja. It wasn't just that this sick man was holding it over her head, trying to make her his sex slave. It was that despite it all, Aja wanted him to do nothing about it. She didn't want his help. She wanted no one's help! Steel couldn't understand it.

Well, whether she wanted it to happen or not, he was taking this into his own hands. Maybe he couldn't kill Joe Snell. But he could hurt him, and hurt him badly. He could make him leave Aja alone.

Steel remembered his younger days. In Texas he'd had enough time and space to let the anger

go. Then in his twenties, he'd
rolled up on the streets of New
York, roaming with an Irish gang.
He'd been a wild thing then, tall,
young, and careless. He couldn't
remember the names of his old
buddies, but he remembered how
long it had taken him to conquer
that rage inside him. And then
once he'd joined the army, there
had been times where the rage
was all he had to keep him going
through these long and bloody
days. When Steel was in a fury
everything in his way became an
opponent; he felt nothing but the
weight of his fists and the angle of
the swing. He'd been a fighter.
No one messed with him.

The army had done a lot to
harness that wildness, but it still
sat inside him like a sleeping

beast. Only once in his sixteen years of service had it woken, and that had cost him his position, but also earned him the respect of a man he admired.

Steel owed everything about his present circumstance to Nigel Burrows. Sergeant Burrows was an old veteran, and Steel's mentor. He was heir to a sizeable fortune; he had no children. He developed lung cancer a year before Steel was discharged. Steel would never forget the call from Burrows' lawyer, informing him of his hero's death, and that Steel was the sole beneficiary of his estate- valued at 57 million dollars.

His life had suddenly changed. The one caveat in Burrows' will:

Steel would only receive the money if he spent a year in isolation. Just one year to clear his head, away from everything, away from the city. He could decide when that year would be, and $100,000 of the fortune would go towards establishing him somewhere, where he could live in modest comfort.

Steel had chosen Boyd. It was an easy decision. He had family ties there.

It made sense for him to come to Boyd, just like it made sense for Aja to take the money he was offering her to get Joe Snell off her tail. He had plenty of cash now, and in a year he would have plenty more, more than he knew what to do with.

She was being stubborn. Absurd.

"Mr. Gray!" A voice broke him from his dark thoughts. He found he'd been standing at the edge of the crowd, perfectly still, his eyes roving over the happy people for a tall man with blue eyes.

Drew Robinson came bounding over, flushed and happy. Steel looked at the boy with new eyes. Hell, he looked just like Aja. He was even dark, like she was. It made the electric blue of his eyes stand out so sharply. Steel had never seen such a strange looking child. He still couldn't grasp that this was Aja's son.

"Hey kid," Steel said gruffly.

"Where's Aja?"

"She's home. You seen the Sheriff anywhere?"

"No," said Drew, looking around. "He ain't here. You looking for him?"

"Yeah," said Steel. "Where are your brothers?" He looked around, but Travis and Daniel weren't where he had last spotted them.

"I dunno," Drew shrugged. "I think they was gonna get a ride over to Washitaw."

"They left you behind?"

The kid shrugged, but Steel could tell he was annoyed at being left behind. "I dunno. Travis told me to go back home. Daniel saw you and said come find you, cus if you was here then Aja had to be here too. Why she ain't with you?"

"Listen, Drew," Steel said, laying a hand on the kid's head. "I need to find the Sheriff."

"Oh. Alright."

He looked at the kid again. For crying out loud. He couldn't just leave him alone.

"Okay, okay. You can come with me."

Drew tried to hide his pleasure. "Okay."

They walked over to Steel's truck and got in.

"I'm about to do something really irresponsible," he told Drew.
 Drew looked at him.

"But I can't take you with me."

"What you mean?" said Drew. "I'm gonna teach a lesson to someone. But you can't come with me, alright?"

Drew stared ahead. Steel examined him from the corner of his eye. He was sure the kid had been smaller, a few months ago when he arrived in Boyd. He'd be a tall man when he grew up, that was certain.

I can't believe this is Aja's son. Was he like his mother? It seemed so. Was he like his father? Only time would tell.

"I'm gonna take you back to stay with your grandpa."

Drew shook his head stubbornly. "Naw, I wanna come with you."

"You can't. I'm not fucking- I'm not playing around, Drew."

"He's gonna throw you in jail."

"This isn't an argument, kid."

"Fine." When he said that, for a moment he sounded exactly like his mother.

They drove back to the Robinsons. Steel let him off at the bottom of the path. Drew jumped out and slammed the door without saying goodbye. Steel immediately regretted letting him go. If he knew Drew Robinson, the kid would be back in town within an hour, by himself, and getting into trouble. Drew didn't mind wandering all over the place alone- a strange trait, for a preteen. *Kind of alarming, but I was the same way*, thought Steel. It wasn't that the kid couldn't handle himself. Steel just didn't trust a Robinson to stay out of trouble in this town.

Well, he'd keep an eye out. He watched Drew stomp inside the house. Steel didn't bother going up again to see if Aja was home.

***

The rest of the day didn't turn out quite like he expected.

As soon as he backed out of the Robinson driveway, the truck blew a tire. He didn't have a spare in the truck bed- he had taken it out to pack roof shingles with Steve Logan-, so he had to hike over to the Tucker place to get it from the shed. He spent a solid forty minutes, red-faced, trying to change the tire. The jack Grandpa Buck loaned him was rusty and useless. Steel had to hike back to the Tucker's again to get a tool box and a jack. The one he usually kept in the truck was missing.

Drew Robinson came out of the house to watch him change the spare. He was sipping a tall glass of lemonade with a straw. The kid had forgotten their prior interaction, and seemed to think the whole tire affair was the funniest thing he'd ever seen. He kept asking Steel questions about the truck, but Steel was short on patience, and told him to beat it.

All of this served to worsen Steel's mood but cool his temper, and by the time he was done he wanted nothing more than to leave the Robinsons' driveway and never return. He drove back to the Tucker ranch, parked the truck, stormed inside, and collapsed on the couch. He had a blinding headache.

***

Aja watched Steel struggle with the truck from her bedroom window. She was still furious with him, but that was slowly melting away. How dare he not realize what she had sacrificed? What she had been through?

She thought of how easily he had offered her the money. She knew should have taken it. Her brothers were more important than her pride. She had a duty to them above everyone else.

But Aja Robinson was tired of everyone owning her. She had relied on herself this long, after her mother had died, to keep everything together. She was worked every day to the bone. She told herself she could pull herself out of this, like she had every other time.

But deep inside, she knew that wasn't true. This was bigger than both of them.

Steel was so brave. So strong. Her protector, her man. She looked at his enormous frame in the driveway, rubbing his temples in frustration, and she couldn't help but smile. He had somehow fit himself in her life. How had that happened so quickly? In just a few months she'd grown to trust him. He'd made a world of a difference with Drew's behavior, Travis's attitude, and Daniel's positivity. He encouraged the boys. He helped them. He taught them. And through it all, she knew he cared about her deeply. Maybe- if she dared to hope- maybe he even loved her.

Yet even that wasn't enough to make her go down there and apologize. Because once she did that, she had to accept his help. And who knew what that would lead to?

Her phone chimed. She closed her eyes, begging for strength and patience. It wasn't Steel. It wasn't her brothers.

Joe: See me tonight. By Wren Hollow. Alone.

***

Steel woke up on the couch on his porch, his mind hazy. His mouth felt sandy, his body caked in sweat. It was mid-afternoon.

He got up to get some water, then came back outside. The afternoon sun had cleared away all the dampness of the morning. Cicadas whined. It was peaceful and sunny and bright.

When he came back outside, he jumped and almost dropped the glass.

An impossibly old woman was sitting on the stump, where he'd first met Grandpa Buck a few months ago. Her hair was white as sugar. She was the smallest old lady he'd ever seen.

"Hello?" He called. She turned to him, and as he approached he saw that her eyes were green as leaves.

"Hi, dear," she drawled in a thick Virginia accent. Her voice was scratchy and rusty, like a bucket of nails. "Sorry to frighten you."

"Can I help you?" Steel wondered if it was common practice for everyone in Boyd to use the Tucker place as a highway.

"No, dear, I'm just resting."

"Okay," said Steel. Her way of speaking reminded him of someone. "Who are you?"

She smiled. Her teeth were stained with tobacco juice. " I live in the mountains. I just like to come down for fourth of July. See the pretty fireworks."

"Do you always come here? To the Tuckers?" Steel wondered if he should be more concerned that a strange old woman was practically sitting on his doorstep. Then he wondered if he was being too inquisitive. Christ, but things did work differently down here. In the North, people lost their heads over trespassing. They were obsessed with fences and walls. Here in Boyd, people wandered all over each other's property and no one seemed to mind.

"Don't worry about me, sugar," She said easily. "I ain't worried about *you*."

Steel looked at her. She was smiling to herself, looking off into the distance.

"What's your name- er- ma'am?"

"Lyn Thompson," she said. "And you are?"

"Steel Gray."

"You look like a Tucker, Steel Gray."

"My mother was a Tucker. Jane Tucker, Fiona's cousin."

"Really." The old woman's eyes sparkled with interest. She gave Steel a once-over.

"You knew her?" Steel asked, surprised.

"Oh, naw. But I knew Fiona, and I knew Fiona's daddy. Yeah- me and Fee were real good friends."

"What was she like?" asked Steel, curious.

"Kind as a flower. But a little soft-she was a sensitive thing. Loved her bible, that she did."

Steel remembered the bible he'd picked up on the dresser of Fiona's room.

"She seemed alright," he conceded. "From what I heard."

"Sure was. Well, I better get going." She clambered to her feet, leaning on a polished wood cane.

"I see God is working through you, Steel Gray," she said. She laid a hand on his arm. Goosebumps raised on his skin; her touch was cool and dry. "Sometimes I see things I'd rather not see; it's a gift and curse, this old age." She patted his arm. "Take care of yourself. You'll see me around again."

He watched her hobble away down the path.

***

The fireworks shot through the whole sky. People came from all over to see them.

Steel felt hollow as he watched them from his porch. He had spent the entire day at the ranch alone, thinking about a hundred different things. The old man's reveal. His argument with Aja. Meeting the strange old woman. He wished he could turn his brain off and get to sleep. He'd wake up tomorrow, still angry, but with a lot more energy.

He got into the truck.

He drove around the town, feeling the air whistle through his hair. He drove around the perimeter of

Boyd, then he drove around it again.

On his second round, his phone chimed. It was Aja.

"Hello?"

"I need your help."

"Where are you?"

"Home."

He picked her up at the end of the driveway. The temperature had plummeted; she was wearing a lilac sweater- her favorite color. Steel remembered her saying once that wearing Lilac made her feel braver- it had been her grandmother's favorite color too. Did she need to be brave tonight?

"Thanks," she said as she climbed in. She smelled like she always did- like vanilla and sugar. Like home.

Steel turned to her and took her face in both hands. She made no move to stop him. He sucked on her lips, pulling and teasing them, and they broke away softly. Her eyes were round and inquisitive.

"What was that for?" she asked.

"For nothing," he said.

"I need your help. He wants to meet tonight. At Wren Hollow. Alone."

She showed him the text.

Steel nodded. "You want me to come with you."

"Yes. I don't know what he's gonna try."

"I'll be there, Aja."

"Thank you," she sighed.

They drove to Wren Hollow, a small, secluded little inlet by the river. It was perfectly dark. Steel shut off the truck engine and they climbed out a little ways before. The singing of crickets and the bawl of bullfrogs made a chorus all the way down to the beach. Steel had Aja walk in front of him. He had wanted her to stay in the car, and check it out himself. But Aja flatly refused; she wouldn't be left alone. No way.

"Remember," he told her. "No one can hurt you when I'm here."

"He's got a gun, Steel."

Steel lifted the hem of his shirt.
Tucked in was an M9 pistol.
Standard issue.

"Oh my God," Aja whispered,
putting a hand to her forehead.
"Please tell me you're not gonna
use that thing."

"I don't want to have to."

Steel felt a sudden prickle up his
spine. He had excellent hearing,
and their eyes were adjusting to
the darkness. The moon was like
a sickle in the sky, giving hardly
any light. He thought he heard
voices.

He ushered Aja into a copse of
trees. "Wait here," he whispered

firmly. "Don't move, okay? Unless I call for help. Then run like hell back to the car." He handed her the keys.

"Put your phone on silent."

He crept down to the beach. It was empty. He walked around the hollow for ten minutes. But there was nothing there but the river, and the trees, and the sounds of the forest. Maybe Joe had just wanted to scare her. If so, he would have done a hell of a good job.

Aja was right where he left her. She practically threw herself into his arms.

"What happened? I didn't hear anything."

"Let's go home," he said, still feeling pins down his spine. "There's no one here."

They rushed back to the car and drove back to his place. Steel could tell Aja was shaken. They went up to his bedroom, and he drew a bath for the both of them in the large porcelain tub. Aja crushed rose petals from the garden and lit candles all around the room. Then they filled it with a special lavender soap Carson had left in the cabinet.

Steel watched Aja undress and climb into the massive tub. Good thing he'd fixed the hot water in time. She undid her hair from the topknot and sank into the water.

Steel watched her for a minute more, then joined her. He let her lean against him. She was soft. The hot water making pearls on her skin and running down her ample breasts.

"You alright?" he murmured.

"Mhhm."

They sat there quietly, content to feel each other's skin on skin. Steel took her breasts and weighed them in his hands. He rubbed her nipples until they hardened and stiffened.

"I need something from you," he said.

"What's that?"

"A Thank You kiss."

They sat in the tub until the water ran cold. They got out and toweled themselves dry.
Aja checked her phone. "The boys are back safe. Grandpa is home."

"Good," said Steel. "So come here."

He cupped her buttocks and pulled her to him, sinking into the bed. They were both naked; she was wet and willing. He slid into her easily, fucking her with slow, deep strokes, enjoying the way her moist hole tightened around him. Slowly he built her to orgasm. She cried out and shuddered, her body shaking in ecstasy, and he poured himself into her, spurting his cream deep in her belly.

Somehow it wasn't enough. He was still hard; he still needed to feel her. He flipped her over and entered her from behind, pulling her up until she was straddling his lap. One hand wrapped gently around her throat, the other reached over to tease her clit. He held her in place as she writhed and moaned against him, pressing his cock deep into her pussy until she begged for a release.

"I'm going to fill you up to the brim again," he whispered in her ear. "I want you to know you're mine."

"Yes, yes sir," Aja whimpered. Her ass bounced against him, but he was the one in control, and she knew it. He let her fall to her knees, her back arched, and continued pumping into her. A wicked thought came into his head. He bent over and pulled her up again, his mouth against her ear. His strokes got faster, more savage. But Aja liked it rough.

"Oh my god," she cried. "Oh..oh."

Steel smiled, his hand tightening around her throat. She liked it when he dominated her, when he showed her who was in control. Only he could bring her to cum like this. Only he knew what she liked.

"Just so you know," he whispered, unloading a final spurt of cum into her needy, sopping pussy, "Next time I see you, I'm taking your asshole next."

CHAPTER FIVE
THE SEARCH

Aja woke up the next morning in Steel's bed. His arm was heavy across her chest; she could hardly breathe. He was a big man for real, she thought, wiggling out from under him as slowly as possible. From experience she knew Steel was a light sleeper. For Aja's mission, she needed him asleep.

She took a moment to look at his big body sprawled across the bed. His hair was a wild golden mane, shot through with streaks of strawberry blonde. Aja could recall the faces of all the Tuckers she had known vividly; people said Steel had the Tucker look, but she personally couldn't see it.

The Tuckers had been big, but fat. Every inch of Steel's body was muscled and proportional. Steel slept on his stomach usually, and he was so tall his feet nearly hung off the end of the bed. Aja remembered the night before with a delicious shudder. She could still feel his seed inside her.

She washed up and brushed her teeth, thinking. He was her protector. She knew in her heart he was the perfect man for her. Big, strong, good with her brothers, honest, like a god in bed. When he touched her, Aja's whole body felt like a live wire; their union was electric. It would be a long while before Aja met another man like Steel. She knew he only had a year in Boyd- he'd let it slip to her earlier. What would happen then? Would she be able to let a man like that go?

Aja bit her lip. She had to convince him to stay. But she also had a duty to her family , and that came first, before anything else.

Aja crept around the room. She'd been in Steel's bedroom before, and she'd figured out that this had to have once been John Tucker's room. The furniture was very old and well-made. The walls were covered in delicate cream paper with brown rose accents. Overall the whole room gave off a masculine aura; the eye was drawn to a large mahogany desk by the window. It was ornately carved, especially the feet, which had been once painted over with gold. She'd never seen such an

273

exquisite piece of craftsmanship. A desk like that in today's market would cost thousands- if you could find anyone to make it. Aja had to wonder where the Tucker family had got their wealth from. Unlike some of the other old Boyd families, they hadn't inherited any local businesses. Their farm was for purely subsistence purposes- her grandfather said they'd never sold anything they grew, in his day. Yes indeed. She had to wonder.

Fiona Tucker would not have kept her diary in here. This was the domain of her father, John, the man she had hated, the man she had feared. Perhaps the Will was in the desk. But Aja got the sense that Steel had searched this room thoroughly already, and exploring

it now was sure to wake him up.
No. Finding it wouldn't be so easy.

She wasn't sure why she was
afraid of Steel waking up and
catching her snooping through his
house. Aja remembered when
Carson Tucker had caught her-
what a mess *that* had been. She
wondered how much Steel knew
about Fiona Tucker's will, and her
family's part in the whole story of
the Tuckers.

Whatever he knew, she wasn't
sticking around to ask him. Aja
trusted Steel. She trusted that he
would protect her. She trusted
that he would protect her family.
But Steel Gray dealt only in
absolutes, he wasn't the type to
appreciate dishonesty or
sneaking- exactly what she was

doing right now. Who knew how he would react if he caught her snooping around the house, looking for some mythical document that would rip his inheritance away from him?

Aja hardened her heart. She decided to start in perhaps the most obvious place- Fiona Tucker's bedroom. Before Steel moved in, she had only been inside the house a few times. It wasn't the friendliest of houses. Steel had done what he could to brighten the place up, but it was still very dark, with austere portraits staring down disapprovingly at every corner. Aja soon realized she had no idea where she was going. It was like the damn place was made of doors. And each one she opened screamed on its hinges like it was a thousand years old.

"Shit," she muttered, when she finally opened what could only be Fiona Tucker's room. It smelled like a tomb. A massive four-poster bed occupied most of it. Aja recalled her grandfather saying that Fiona Tucker had been bedridden in the last few months of her life. To Aja, that pointed to the will being hidden somewhere in that very room. Fiona surely hadn't traversed the entire three-story house to hide it.

Or had she? Aja checked under the bed. Remembering the Nancy Drew novels she'd read as a kid, she kept an eye out for secret compartments and hidden trapdoors. The room was so dusty. She rummaged through the desk, noting that though the whole room was as neat as a pin, the contents of the desk were disorganized. Perhaps someone had been here before her, searching frantically for the same thing she was. Interesting.

There was nothing in the desk. Aja ran her fingertips under it, lightly, lightly. Maybe there would be a secret compartment, a latch, anything…

Her eyes rolled to the ceiling; she sighed. Nothing. Of course.

There was no other furniture in the room but an old armoire, which had nothing but some frilly undergarments, yellow with age, and a scrapbook resting on top of it. Nothing. Aja felt foolish and angry. She had believed her grandfather when he told her about the will. She had wanted to believe. Was it just delusion? Was it wrong for her to feel so hopeful about this money- money that she wasn't truly entitled to?

She flipped through the scrapbook idly. It was mostly pictures of Fiona from her childhood- familiar places in Boyd, with faces Aja didn't know. She wondered if Fiona Tucker had ever left this town. Aja didn't think so. A leaf of paper fell out when she pulled the scrapbook off the drawer. Aja turned it over.

It was dated- from several months ago. It read:

"Turn away from evil and do good; so shall you dwell forever. For the

Lord loves justice; he will not forsake his saints. They are preserved forever, but the children of the wicked shall be cut off. The righteous shall inherit the land and dwell upon it forever."
Psalms 37:21.

It was written in flowing, loose script. A woman's hand. Aja felt the hair on the back of her neck raise to attention. Written under the inscription was the following :

Trust in Christ Jesus. Look to His cradle, where the Son of God first laid his crown.. - Fiona Mae Tucker.

"Now what are you doing?"

Aja screamed and dropped the scrapbook. Her heart was bursting out of her chest; but it was only Steel. He was shirtless, leaning tiredly in the door frame, looking both irritated and amused.

"I- I'm sorry!" She gasped. She picked up the scrapbook and hastily replaced it. What the hell did it all mean?

"It's okay," he said, eyeing her funnily. "Were you looking for something?"

"Nope," she said evenly. "Nothing in particular."

Steel was silent for a few seconds. His blue eyes seemed to pierce her soul. Then his gaze shifted; turned appraising. Aja wore a thin nightshirt- one of his. Her brown nipples poked through. In the excitement they had raised to attention. She felt his eyes linger on her round hips, on her breasts, on the way the thin fabric clung to each of her curves invitingly. Aja's breath grew shallow. She knew what it meant when Steel looked at her that way.

"Come here," he said.

She obeyed. Steel could make her forget everything in a moment. She loved it. She loved how he could command her. How small she felt next to him, so exposed but so utterly safe...

Steel folded her in his arms, turning her around so her ass was pressed against the hard length of his erection. He rubbed it between her cheeks, letting her feel it. "Mmm," he murmured in her hair. "I thought you'd left."

"Nuh-uh," she whispered, smiling. She forgot everything from before- it felt so good to be in Steel's arms, inhaling his wonderful manly scent, feeling his heat against her...

He spun her back around to face him. A wicked smile played across his lips. Aja felt a flare of unease.

"Remember what I said?" Steel murmured. One hand cupped her chin firmly, pulling her gaze up to meet his.

"Huh?" She replied, puzzled.

One arm held her fast, pinning her arms to her side. His other hand crept under the hem of her nightshirt. He skimmed a finger through her pussy lips; Aja gasped. His gaze never broke from hers. He was delving in her pussy, bringing out her cream with two fingers. One finger began to lightly circle the rim of her most secret entrance...

"I said," Steel said, putting his lips against her ear. "I'd be taking your asshole next. You've never been taken in the ass, have you, Aja?"

Aja felt her legs turn to water. Her stomach was fluttering. Did he mean it? Was she ready to take him...?

"Answer me," he commanded softly. One finger started to push into her asshole, wet with her pussy cream. She whimpered.

"N-no," she whispered. It felt...so good. It felt so good.

"Good," Steel said. "I can tell. You're gonna be tight as a virgin."

He began to finger-fuck her asshole, still holding her pinned to his body. He could feel her breasts heavy and peaky with desire. It would be so easy to turn her over this bed right now, and just slide into her pussy. Steel admitted it was one of his favorite positions. He liked having Aja bent over, arched on his dick, where he could watch her ass bounce from the best view of all.

But this wasn't the place. He slid his finger from her anal passage. "Go upstairs, babygirl. Undress, " he whispered. "Don't make me wait."

Aja did as she was told. When Steel joined her in the bedroom she was nude. Ready for him.

"On your knees," he murmured softly. Aja complied. A bead of precum was leaking from the tip of his tumescent pole. She tasted his salty sweetness, the musky odor of his groin filling her nose. Steel was a big man, not overly long but very girthy. She stretched her lips to accommodate his meaty staff, feeling him thrust past her tongue to the back of the throat. Steel liked to hold her head steady as he pumped her mouth. Her mouth was like another pussy for him to use at his pleasure, and Aja could somehow take him all down her throat, a feat which drove him insane. As he pumped in and out of her mouth, he appreciated how full her lips were, how they slobbered and gagged on his cock so beautifully, the way a woman's lips were meant to. He liked her to suck on his balls- almost as much as he liked cumming down her throat. Sometimes he liked to grab her hair and just plow into the back of her mouth until his balls were empty and aching. Maybe another time, he thought idly. He had other holes he wanted to try.

"Turn around," he commanded. She bent over the edge of the bed. Aja's eyes were round with anticipation- maybe a little apprehensive, too. Steel reminded himself that this was her first time. As badly as he wanted to pummel her tiny brown asshole with no reservations, he had to remember she had never done this before...

"Spread your pussy for me, babygirl," he said, slapping her ass. Hard. "Let me see." Aja squealed and did so. She was creamy all over. It was dripping down her thighs.

"You like sucking my dick?" He murmured, plying her pussy again for the cream. Aja's pussy was the wettest Steel had ever fucked. It was heaven. He liked cumming inside her and watching their mixed juices leak out of her pussy.

"Tell me." He pumped her with his fingers. God. Even just plowing her with her fingers, he could tell how tight she was. Her pussy could suck him dry for every drop of cum he had. Steel had planned to take her asshole first, but with so much cream filling up her pussy, it would be a waste not to dip his cock in it.

"I like...uh.."

"Like what? Getting on your knees? Sucking my cock?"

"Yes, sir," she whispered. He slid just the tip of his cock into her as a reward. Her wetness was overwhelming. Already he wanted to shoot his load.

"But you like when I fuck you more," he said. Aja was trying to angle her hips, get more of his cock inside her. Greedy girl. He held her firmly in place.

"You'll get enough of that when I fuck you in the ass," he said. She was practically fighting to take his dick. Her pussy was tighter than ever but she wanted to fit it in, she wanted him to fill her up. Hard to believe such a good girl could be so cock hungry. "Be patient baby."

Aja groaned. "Please...uh. Please," she whimpered.

"Please what?"

"Please, sir."

"Please fuck you more?"

"Yes..Yes!"

He could see her asshole tensing as he plumbed her pussy with his thick tool. He couldn't wait to ravage it. Her slick, swollen lips rode his dick until she was crying out in pleasure. Steel grunted. Fuck. He shot rope after rope of cum straight into her womb. Hearing her cry out in orgasm drove him even further. He pulled out of her and was still hard as iron. Perfect.

"Your ass is next," he told her.

"Yes, sir," Aja breathed. He patted her ass, pleased with her eagerness. They moved up on the bed and Aja laid flat on her stomach. "Good girl. Spread it open for me again baby. Let me see it."

Aja's asshole was little and tight. He worked a finger in her pussy, then used to juices to probe her asshole open. She would fit all of him- she had to. It would be her first ass-fucking, but she'd enjoy it.

Aja was nervous at first but his finger felt amazing. She couldn't believe she was doing it in her most secret hole. Once the head of Steel's cock began to push at her tight entrance, she only had to breathe and relax. He fit the head past. He used their juices to lubricate him and slide in easier. The tightness of her asshole drove him mad, but he wanted her to feel good too.

Slowly, achingly slowly, he began to plow her asshole. The brown cherry took him all the way to the balls. She was soft and tight and pliable. Aja, for her part, could hardly believe Steel was invading such a forbidden hole. And she was loving it. She loved the way his balls slapped against her ass, the way his invading cock stimulated her most sensitive parts.

He reached under her to rub a thumb on her clit, which was already at full attention. His thrusting made her enormous buttocks bounce. What made him so crazy was the fact that Aja was in fact a good girl- a good girl, getting her ass fucked in his bed. Her brown skin contrasted against his dick nicely, emphasizing the way they were joined. Steel imagined her in a hundred different positions, each one with his thick pole up her asshole, reminding her that every hole was his to use and cum inside. He'd taken her mouth and her pussy, and now her ass. He was sodomizing her, and she was loving it. Her cries turned to pants and gasps as he punished her clit and pushed her to the brink of orgasm.

"Steel! Cum in me, cum in my asshole, please..."

Steel could take it no longer. He grabbed her waist and began to fuck her asshole in earnest, sawing in and out of her pleasurable hole. Aja couldn't be any tighter. He spewed his load inside her tush, grunting, watching her juicy brown ass bounce on his cock to take every last drop. Aja didn't waste any cum. He withdrew and had her hold her ass open for his pleasure, as he watched his seed leak from her ass and pussy at the same time. She had been well-used.

"Good girl," he groaned. "That's my girl."

He pulled her into his arms. He couldn't believe she'd done so well, taking all of him into that tiny asshole of hers. They were both exhausted. Aja pushed her face into his chest, trembling from a lingering orgasm.

Her phone rang.

It was the Sheriff.

Steel felt anger rise up in him, along with, unbelievably, his erection. "Pick it up," he said.

Aja looked at him, and back at the phone, hesitating.

"Pick it up, babe."

She did, and he slid his throbbing cock into her asshole again as soon as she answered. This time he didn't go slow. He fucked her hard, wanting her to reach the heights of pleasure.

"Ahh...Ahh...Hello?" She gasped. She reached a hand under to play with her clit again. Steel grinned.

"Aja? Is that you?" Snapped the Sheriff.

"Shit...yeah, it is. What...uhhnn....what do you want?"

"Tell him," Steel said wickedly, leaning over to whisper in her ear. He might have whispered a little too loud. "Tell him you're getting fucked in the ass."

"What the fuck is going on?" Joe spat. "You damn slut. Where were you the other night?"

"Hey Joe?" said Aja.

"What?"

"Leave me the hell alone. I'm busy."

She laughed in surprise at herself, and hung up the phone. Steel tossed it on the other side of the bed and came again into her ass- not as hard as before, but it shook them both to the core. He felt his love for Aja beating through every vein in his body. God, the girl had a wicked sense of humor, one that came out in the strangest ways.

"God, woman," he gasped, half in laughter, half in exhaustion.

"What?" Aja said, clutching her sides. She could feel Steel's seed gushing out of her. The feeling of his dick inside her lingered. She felt happy. Who cared about the Sheriff?

"I love you. You're one in a million."

"I love you too," Aja sighed, wiping tears from her eyes. She couldn't remember feeling so blessed, and so blissful and protected, in a long time. She had a man who loved her, and a man she loved right back.

And maybe, she thought secretly, as she stroked Steel's velvety curls, she was one step closer to unlocking the mystery of Fiona Tucker's Will.

***

"Shit," swore Daniel Robinson. It was high afternoon. The sun was beating down on his neck, and trails of sweat crawled down his spine like insects. His T-shirt stuck fast to his torso.

Daniel was swearing not because of the heat, but because of the brown pickup truck that had just pulled into the parking lot.

The boys were on the border between the two counties, by the Fell's bridge. It was only a couple miles from their place. The Robinson boys were used to walking.

"Travis," he muttered. "Tell me you ain't pull some crap over in Washitaw."

"Why?" asked his brother, looking up from his phone. His eyes fell on the truck, and widened. "Aw hell."

"Let's go," said Daniel urgently.

Travis stood up, fists clenched. "I ain't scared of him."

"You think I care? Let's go!" Daniel barked at his brother.

The door to the truck opened and three men got out. They wore camouflage jackets, even in the heat, aviator sunglasses, and baseball caps. One had a rifle slung across his shoulder. He was tall, with curly brown hair and an all-too familiar sneer.

Travis saw the rifle and the man holding it. A thrill of fear flared in his throat. The men were talking casually to each other outside the truck, but Daniel knew it was a power play; they wanted to see if the boys would run.

"Run," he told Travis. "I think that's Dean Murphy."

Travis looked from his brother to the men. "We can't outrun 'em, Danny."

"Then start walking," said Daniel. He pulled his younger brother's arm. Travis followed. The boys moved as fast as they could without running. The men saw them and laughed. They made no move towards them, but Daniel wasn't taking any chances.

He fumbled for his phone. It was out of battery- dead.

"Travis," he said frantically. "Gimme your phone."

"Who you gonna call?" said Travis. Daniel had always been the most level-headed of his brothers; it scared him to hear the fear in his voice.

"I'm gonna call the ghostbusters," he snapped. "Mr. Gray, obviously."

"Call Aja," Travis said. Daniel ignored him and dialed Steel's number, thanking God for the umpteenth time that his memory was so powerful. He knew all the numbers in his phone by heart.

Steel picked up on the third ring. "Hey kid."

"Come get us," Daniel said quickly. "We're in trouble."

Steel was immediately in military mode. "Where are you?"

"Fell's Point," Daniel said. "Oh hell. Travis. They're getting in the truck."

"What color is the truck?"

"Uh...brown. Rusty. Toyota '00, I think."

Travis cursed, pulling on Daniel's sleeve. "Hang up and let's go over the bridge."

"Daniel," Steel said calmly from the other end. "Who is it? Who's after you?"

"Joe, Dean Murphy, and I don't know the other guy."

"Stay on the phone," Steel said. "I'm coming."

Travis snatched the phone away. "They're driving towards us!"

The two boys broke into a run.

***

Steel and Aja had been in the garden. Steel was showing her his plans for a peach orchard- an idea that Carson had enthusiastically endorsed. They'd spent the rest of the morning discussing plans for the property, with Aja dropping hints that she wanted him to help her with some landscaping around hers. They'd been feeling light and happy, enjoying each other's company. Aja expected that her brothers would be out all day. She'd checked in on all of them just a couple hours ago. Drew and Grandpa Buck were home watching TV. And Travis was out with Daniel- which meant he was staying out of trouble.

Or so she'd thought.

Steel was already halfway to the car by the time Daniel hung up, and Aja close behind. She was frantic with worry, but as always, she kept it under a tight seal of calm.

"Dean Murphy?" Steel asked. "Billy and Steve's friend?"

"He's a piece of work," Aja said bitterly. Her voice trembled. She wished Steel could go faster, pedal to the floor, though they were a good fifteen miles above the speed limit. They were still five minutes away. Anything could happen in five minutes. Especially where Joe Snell and Dean Murphy were concerned. "A real slimy guy."

"Explain," said Steel, grabbing her hand. She had been tapping her fingers on her thigh frantically.

"A couple years ago- like I'm talking, six or seven- there was some incident in Washitaw," Aja explained. "A Mexican kid turned up in the river. Wrapped in barbed wire." She shut her eyes tightly. She couldn't think about that. Everything would be fine.

"Jesus God," Steel swore.

"They never found out who did it," Aja told him. "But you know, Boyd's small, and Washitaw isn't that much bigger. There were rumors…"

"What rumors?"

"That Joe helped cover it up. And that Dean Murphy did it."

"Help me understand," Steel said. He couldn't believe this was happening. He remembered watching Dean Murphy play cards with the men at the Birdcage, all those months ago. He'd seemed like an irritable but genuinely decent fellow. It was hard to reconcile that image with the gruesome story Aja was telling him. That poor kid..

"Why?" Steel asked. But he knew, from years' experience, that sometimes there didn't have to be a why. Sometimes people didn't need a reason.

"They said the kid cussed at him," Aja said shakily, thinking of Travis' foul mouth and lack of filter. She'd been telling him for ages. *Stand your ground, but be respectful. You don't want to give people 'round here a reason.* "But they also said he tried to steal from Dean Murphy. Something about drugs. Murphy's a sensitive guy. But I don't know. It was...it was hard to get the truth." She was breathing slowly and deeply, but her legs were completely numb and she felt on the verge of tears.

"Why would they be targeting your brothers?" Steel asked. They were minutes away.

"Travis was messin' with Dean Murphy's daughter," Aja said.

"That's gotta be the reason. God damn it."

"We'll find them," Steel promised her. "We're almost there."

"Please, Steel," Aja whispered. She put her head in her hands. Would they get there in time? If something happened to her brothers, she'd never forgive herself.

***

"Where y'all goin', boys?" called Joe Snell, leaning out the passenger side window. Daniel kept an iron grip on his brother's bicep. He could tell Travis' temper was simmering; his brother reacted like a wild animal when cornered. He lashed out violently. The last thing either of them needed was to give these redneck thugs a reason to get physical.

Stay calm, Daniel told himself. He'd always believed that his intelligence could get him out of any trouble. But only to a point. Travis was the better smooth-talker, but right now he didn't dare trust Travis to open his mouth. He'd have to take charge.

"Home, sir," he choked out. *Sir.* He had to call them *sir.*

"Walkin pretty quick," drawled the Sheriff. He gestured to the driver and they pulled over, right in front of the boys. Daniel started to step around the truck, but the doors opened, and the men piled out. They were cornered, on this lonely highway with not a soul in sight. Nowhere to run. Nowhere to go.

Every nerve in his body prepared to fight. Travis was a coil of tension and fury, waiting for someone to touch him and set it loose. Daniel struggled to hold on to his cool. He wouldn't beg these bastards, but he couldn't let them hurt his little brother either.

"Let us through," he demanded. Travis said nothing.

"It ain't you I got beef with, boy," snapped Dean Murphy. He pointed at Travis. "It's him. You. Ain't I tell you to leave my daughter alone?"

Travis said nothing. Daniel raised his hands in contrition. *You just need to stall. Steel is coming.*

"My brother doesn't know what you're talking about."

"Shut the fuck up, kid. Your brother's got a Goddamn tongue in his head, ain't he? Speak up!" Dean Murphy barked. The third man lit a cigarette and took a deep drag. He looked bored. Joe Snell stroked the barrel of his rifle. "What were you doing with Susie yester' night?"

"I dunno what you're talking about," Travis spat finally. "I never touched that girl a lick more than she wanted. And you know it."

Dean advanced towards Travis; Daniel stepped in front of his brother.

Dean Murphy was not a small man. One swat sent Daniel spinning too the ground. It took him forever to fall, but only a second to spring back up to his feet again. His head rang but adrenaline was pumping through his veins. Warm, hot liquid gushed down his chin, and a sharp pain blazed in the center of his face. Blood. His nose was broken.

Travis's reaction was instant. He leapt on Dean Murphy, and Dean Murphy leapt on Travis. Joe seized Daniel and pinned his arms behind his back in a wrestler's hold. It was so painful Daniel cried out, which only incensed Travis more.

The third man pointed the rifle at Travis's head. "Back off."

Travis released his hold on Dean Murphy's shirt. Daniel was panting. Blood was dripping from his nose and falling in the dust, drop by drop.

"What do you want?" Travis demanded. He just wanted Joe to let go of Daniel. It looked like his brother was having trouble breathing. A high, desperate note crept into his voice. What were these psychopaths planning?

"Leave Susie alone," snapped Dean, flexing his hands into fists. He wiped the spittle from his mouth. "Or I swear to God…"

"Swear to God what?" taunted Travis. His temper was loose now and there was no holding it back. But he was much smaller than these men. Any wrong move…

"You're gonna kill me? Lock me up for some shit I didn't do? Let him *go*, damn it!" He moved to pull Daniel away, but Snell danced away from his hands.

Daniel was snorting and choking on the blood that had filled his mouth. Joe had him in a headlock, his head tilted up to the sky. He forced the boy to his knees.

Travis launched himself at Joe, only to be pulled back forcefully by Dean and thrown to the ground hard. The barrel of the rifle dug into his guts. "Move again and Rick here is gonna fill your ass with lead," Dean hissed. "We're gonna teach you lil' coons a lesson today about manners."

He nudged Travis to his feet. They frog-marched both boys towards the truck. *Get in that truck and you both die,* Travis told himself. *Steel isn't coming.*

"Let him go," he said to Joe. His brother was fighting for consciousness. Travis felt desperate. "He ain't do nothing. Let him go."

"Shut up," snapped Joe.

Dean laughed. "I didn't hear a please."

"Travis, shut *up*," Daniel choked out. He wasn't about to leave his brother alone with these monsters.

They pushed Travis to his feet. "Please," he gritted.

Rick slammed the rifle in the back of Travis's head. Again he fell to the ground; he caught himself just in time from crashing into the asphalt. His vision was a cosmic blur of red and green and yellow. He wanted to vomit; he fought back the urge.

"Come on, Dean. We're wastin' time. Let's take care of 'em here," said Rick.

"Get 'em in the truck first."

***

Steel and Aja drove around Fell's Point for a solid minute. They saw no trace of the boys or anyone else. It looked like a quiet fishing spot on the river, not exactly the type of spot for two young kids to spend an afternoon. Steel wondered what the hell Daniel and Travis had been doing out here.

Aja was frantic with fear, but she was hiding it extremely well. Steel appreciated how her composure never slipped. He reflected that Aja would have probably done well in the army.

"I don't see them," Steel said calmly. It wouldn't do any good to show Aja his own nervousness. "We'll drive up aways, try to spot the car."

"Maybe they're by the river," Aja said quietly.

"I'll get out to look."

"Steel." Aja said.

"Yeah?"

"Do you have a gun?"

"I do, babe. But if Joe Snell is there, I better not use it."

Aja nodded. "I'm coming with you."

Steel parked the car on a shoulder and climbed out. His face was dark. "Absolutely not." Aja climbed out anyway. She had to be sure her brothers were alright. And she wanted to make sure Joe Snell would never mess with her or her family ever again.

***

They checked by the river. They drove up the road. There was nothing but emptiness; the day was so hot that most people were inside. The beauty of the day seemed to mock them; Aja wondered how it could look so fine when she was filled to the brim with terror. She wished for thunder and lightning, rain, anything but the cloudless, sunny sky, and the nasal whine of cicadas. Today was a day for watermelon and picnics, for fishing and sleeping under magnolia trees. She couldn't get the image of her brothers dead and floating down the Wilminac river out of her mind. When they'd pulled the Mexican kid out a few years ago, blue crabs had eaten his tongue and eyes. He'd been completely naked, mauled beyond recognition by the barbed wire. She'd heard they'd only been able

to identify him by the gold cross
he wore around his neck.

They looked everywhere. Aja had
fallen silent. Her face was drawn.

"We should have called the
police," Steel said.

"Dean Murphy is the police chief
in Washitaw," Aja said tonelessly.
"And Joe is the Sheriff. You don't
know how things work around
here, Steel. You don't know how
deep it goes."

"Don't give up," Steel said firmly.
They were headed back to the
car; it had only taken him a
minute to rush down and scan the
river. No sign of anything but the
bubbling of catfish, and the swarm
of river flies.

When they got to the car, someone was waiting for them.

It was the old, white-haired woman Steel had seen on his property on the Fourth of July. Lyn Thompson. She wore the exact same clothes she'd been wearing then, and was holding the cane in front of her as she leaned against his car.

"You?" Steel said. He stepped in front of Aja instinctively.

"Well it ain't the Queen of England, honey," the woman cackled.

"We don't have the time, Ma'am. We're in a hurry."

"I know where the boys are," said the old woman quickly. Her voice sounded like a bucket of nails. "I saw them take them up a piece. Back into Boyd."

"You did?" Aja cried. "Where?"

"Take me with you, I'll show you."

"It's not safe, ma'am."

"Pardon me, sonny, but kiss my ass," the lady said. "You wanna find these boys or not?"

They all piled in Steel's truck. Lyn Thompson climbed in the passenger's seat. "Who was with them?" Aja pressed.

"I only know one of 'em," she said. "Dean Murphy. And there was a tall handsome fella, and a short and ugly one."

Well, that wasn't new information. But she seemed to know where she was going. They drove back into Boyd.

"Stop here," said Lyn suddenly.

"Do you see them?"

"No. They're a quarter mile up the road. In the forest where the old church used to be. They ain't got too far yet, and your boys are alright."

"How do you know?" Aja demanded. She was still baffled at the sudden appearance of this ancient woman, whom she had never seen before in all her years in Boyd, but who Steel seemed to know. She was even more confused by the niggling sense in her heart that she had met this woman before.

"I just know," said the woman firmly. Steel stopped the truck and she climbed out. "And a word of caution, girlie," Lyn said before she closed the door, staring piercingly at Aja. "Whatever it is you're looking for, it's not in the Tucker House."

Aja wouldn't have been more surprised if the woman told her she was indeed the Queen of England. But before she could get a word out, Lyn Thompson banged the door shut and Steel peeled away.

"What the hell?" Aja said, staring.

"I don't know what *that* was about," said Steel as they sped up the road. "But I think we found your brothers."

Sure enough, as Lyn Thompson had described, the brown truck was parked on a shoulder of the road a quarter mile up, right where a tiny, almost invisible path opened into the forest. Over a hundred years ago, the land had belonged to another Boyd family, the Kesenberrys. They had been Quakers, holding worship sessions . Steel remembered reading about the abandoned Quaker church in *The Complete History of Boyd County*, a book Carson had laying about at the Tucker House. The Kesenberrys had been run out of town in the 1930's, and the church burned to cinders. But the foundation still remained- Steel recalled seeing a picture of it in the book.

He surveyed the brown truck quickly, memorizing the license plate.

"Stay in the car, Aja, baby. Please."

"Absolutely not," she replied. Her face was screwed in determination. She had no weapon but her fury. But fury alone wasn't enough. Steel didn't intend to let her get in the way or get hurt.

"Then let's move," he told Aja. "Quickly."

Aja was already way ahead of him. Steel drew his gun. They jogged along the path.

"I hear voices," Aja said. Her heart was in her throat.

"Don't show yourself yet," Steel told her. "You hear me? These men are dangerous and they can hurt you. You're no good to the boys if they-"

"I know!" Aja snapped. "Alright."

A gunshot pierced the air, stirring the forest birds into flight, and echoing through the woods. A high scream of pain rode on the waves of it, and then all was still and silent.

CHAPTER SIX
OUT FOR BLOOD

The truck belonged to Dean
Murphy, but the gun was Joe
Snell's. It was a Marlin hunting
rifle, designed to penetrate flesh
but not spray on impact and spoil
the game. Almost every man in
Boyd owned a rifle like that. There
were worse weapons to be shot
with, but in that moment,
perspective wasn't exactly on
Travis Robinson's mind. He
stared at the hole in his chest, at
the bright red blood seeping out of
it. His mind didn't register the
pain; it came from far away, like a
cloud floating down from the sky
and descending in a shower of
red mist.

"Travis! Travis!" Daniel screamed. He struggled against his bonds; Joe had zip-tied his hands together. "You bastards! You sons of bitches!"

Joe stared at Rick. "Dumbass," he drawled. "I told you not to shoot so close to the road."

Dean Murphy spat a knot of tobacco juice. Travis had sank to the ground. He was holding a hand over the hole in his chest. It made Dean happy to hear the boy wheezing, trying not to scream. That would show him and his smart ass mouth.

"Let's finish this up, then," he said, pulling the hunting knife from his belt. "Show this shithead what happens when you step above your station. That's the problem with you black-"

"Finish up what?" Steel said coldly, stepping into the clearing. Rick swung the rifle at him, Steel fired instinctively, with all the years of his training behind him. The shot caught the man in the elbow, shredding through the bone. He shrieked and dropped the gun, which went off again, booming through the forest.

Joe moved towards Steel.

"I don't think so," Steel snapped, firing at his feet. Both Dean and Joe went absolutely still. Daniel had started to crawl towards his brother,

"Well," Dean licked his lips. "If it ain't Mr. Texas."

Aja, unable to hold back, burst through the forest line. Travis was groaning on the ground, still bleeding profusely.

"Jesus," laughed Joe. Steel detected a hint of nervousness behind his voice. This had somehow gone completely off the rails, and it didn't look good for him.

"Take him away, Aja," Steel said, glancing at Travis and his weeping brother. "Take him to the hospital."

Joe's blue eyes widened. "She can't drive."
"I can now," Aja said. Her voice was shaking. She helped her middle brother up. Daniel hobbled to his feet, his hands still locked

together. Rick was delirious on the ground; Steel's shot had nearly taken off his arm.

Aja walked up to him. "He's the one who shot Travis?"

Steel nodded. With a viciousness he had never seen from her before, Aja drew her foot back and kicked the man squarely in the bullet wound. He made an animal sound that chilled everyone that heard it, and fainted The clearing went deadly quiet. There was blood all over Aja's tennis shoe.

"Throw those away," Steel directed. She couldn't speak; she only nodded. Holding the gun with one hand, Steel tossed her his pocket knife. She sliced the zip ties off Daniel. He limped to Steel's side.

"I want to stay with Travis."

"He'll be alright," Steel assured him. "If Aja gets out of here in time."

"Steel-" Aja began.

"He stays," said Steel firmly. Daniel was the only one of them who was fine- his nose had stopped bleeding, and blood was crusted on his lips and chin, but he was physically fine. Aja looked at Steel in alarm, but he was firm. "I'll be right after you."

As Aja left, Steel turned to Joe. "Whatever problem you had with Aja, you should have left her brothers out of it."

"Brothers," sneered Joe. "One of them is my own son."

"He needs a doctor," Dean said, looking at Rick. He was still out cold, clutching the shredded remains of his right arm.

"Worry about yourself," Steel snapped. A hardness he hadn't felt in months- maybe years- was icing over his heart. He couldn't get the image of Travis's blood out of his mind, of the defeated, terrified look on Daniel's face. He remembered just a day ago when both boys had been laughing and happy. He turned back to Joe, death in his heart.

"Drew Robinson is your son."

"Of course," Joe spat. "Who else?"

"Pat Tucker?"

"I'll spare you the details of our night with little Aja Robinson," Joe said. He looked murderous, far from the wicked mask of composure he'd had when he first visited Steel at the Tucker House. "But yes, Drew is my son."

"Why did you go after the boys?" Steel directed the question to Dean. Where Joe looked like he would snap in fury at any second, Dean was trying his best to look contrite and apologetic. Playing innocent, the wounded father. Steel wasn't buying it for a second.

Dean licked his lips again. "He went after my daughter, Susie."

"What do you mean?"

"He forced himself on her."

"That's a damn lie," said Daniel furiously, speaking up for the first time. "I was there. I heard her ask him to leave. I heard her say she wanted to-"

"Liar!" roared Dean, composure slipping. "I wouldn't believe a damn coon if it told me the grass was green. You expect me to believe-"

"Enough," Steel cut in coldly. "What did your daughter say? What did she tell you?"

"She didn't have to tell me nothin'. I saw him drop her home, that night. Kissing her, feelin' her. No way a daughter of mine would do such a thing unless he forced her, and that's the God-blamed truth."

Daniel shook his head in disbelief. His eyes were sparking. He wanted to snatch the gun from Steel's hands and empty it into Dean Murphy's stomach. "You were gonna kill my brother."

"Nothing the brat didn't deserve," said Joe. "And as for *you*...you're gonna have a tough time getting into college from the Virginia State prison."

"You think you're making any arrests today?" Steel said. The depths of this man's arrogance would shock a politician.

"You're holding two officers of the law at gunpoint," Joe said, puffing out his chest. "I don't see how either of you walk out of this. You can't kill us and you can't set us free. So what's it gonna be, cowboy?"

"I *can* kill you, actually," said Steel. His voice was flat and hard. "Very, very easily."

"Steel, he's right," said Daniel miserably. "We have to let them go."

"Hold the gun, Daniel." He handed the revolver to the boy.

"What? Why-"

In one fluid motion, Steel launched himself at Joe Snell. They were almost of a height, but Steel had almost fifty pounds on him, and all the fury of the last six months pent up behind his fists. Joe had clearly not been expecting an attack; he went down like a sack of corn. As Dean Murphy watched, astounded, Steel rolled and got the other man under his hips, straddling him. Then it was just a matter of strength. He had plenty of that. It was too easy. He let himself sink into the rage, his muscles moving with years' worth of memory. He thought of Travis, of Drew, and of sweet, angelic Aja. This sick beast had violated her, had fathered a child on her. He was beyond forgiveness. Steel was avenging her.

His fists sailed through the air like hammers, pounding Joe Snell's face beyond recognition. There was silence in the forest, just the moans of Joe, the grunting of Steel Gray, and the sick sound of slapping flesh.

"Stop," Daniel said weakly. "Mr. Gray! Steel! Stop it! Stop it!"

Steel pulled away and got to his feet. The skin on his knuckles was torn. But Joe's face had taken the real damage. Pieces of his teeth were embedded in Steel's fists. He hardly felt it. He stood over the man like an angel of death, his hair floating around his face like a golden halo. Daniel couldn't see his expression.

"We need to get back," Daniel whispered. The man Rick was starting to wake up again.

"You're right," panted Steel. "Let's go."

He turned to Dean Murphy. The man raised his hands in surrender. The look on Steel's face was terrifying, but his tone was soft. He had just thought of something.

"P-please," Dean stammered.

"Did you kill that Mexican boy?"

"W-what?"

"The boy they found six years ago, in the Washitaw. Wrapped in the barbed wire. Was it you?"

Dean's eyes rolled around. Looking for backup that wasn't there, would never come. Steel's lip curled. If he had to take a guess, he figured this man was the kind of bully that never fought his battles alone.

"Answer honestly," said Steel.
"I didn't kill him," Dean croaked. "But I drove the car."

Steel nodded. "Why?"

"Is that what this is about?" Dean said incredulously, his voice trembling. "Some kid?"

"Answer me," Steel grated.

"He said something we didn't like. Needed...to teach him a lesson."

"I see."

"Let's go," Daniel urged.

"Your careers are finished," Steel promised. Joe Snell was still conscious; he gave the message to the both of them. "You have no idea who you're dealing with. If you come near Aja or any of the Robinson boys again, it'll be your ass in the fire."

"Alright," Dean Murphy breathed.

"And just know," Steel said coldly, "I don't leave loose ends."

He picked up the rifle that the man had dropped, and unloaded all the bullets in Daniel's shirt. Then the two of them made to leave. Joe was finally sitting up, a line of red drool trailing from his mouth. His jaw was distended, hanging grotesquely to his chest. *Wonder if we look alike now*, Steel thought viciously. He walked up to the man, who backed away.

"One more thing. Aja owes you nothing. You're gonna forget about asking her for money. You'll never call or speak to her again. Hear me?"

His eyes brimming with hate, Joe Snell nodded.

They made to leave. "Take care of that man," Steel said to Dean, jutting his chin toward Rick. "I think that has to amputate."

***

Steel and Daniel hung back in the woods. Steel called Aja while they waited for Dean, Joe and Rick to limp out towards the brown truck.

"Babe," he said when she answered. He could practically

feel her sigh of relief. "Yes. I'm alright. Daniel is with me. He's alright too. How's Travis?"

"They just sent him into surgery," Aja said. "I didn't know what to tell them. They keep asking me about it. They want to call the police. What do I do?"

Steel thought about it. "Would the police help?"

"No. No, I don't think so."
"Say it was a hunting accident."

"You sure? What if they don't believe me?"

"Come pick us up. We're waiting for them to leave. We're still in the forest."

"Are you sure?"

"We'll go straight back to the hospital, Aja. There's nothing we can do for Travis except pray."

"I'm coming."

***

They waited for Aja quietly, hidden by the broad trees that skirted the edge of the road. They saw the three men- Rick being supported by Dean, Joe walking drunkenly, holding his jaw- clamber into the truck. Steel guessed they were going to the hospital too. He didn't want Aja there alone when they arrived.

"I can't believe this," said Daniel. "I can't believe all this happened."

"You alright?" Steel asked, eyeing him.

"I've got a headache."

"How's your nose?"

"Better. I thought it was broken. But it's not."

"I guess that won't be the last we'll hear of Sheriff Joe," said Steel grimly. "Somethin' tells me that man doesn't know when to quit."

"He's been doing this for years," said Daniel. "It got worse when you arrived." He furrowed his brow, as if working up the courage to ask something.

"Spit it out," Steel said. "I'm getting constipated just looking at you."

"Is it true what he said? He's Drew's dad?"

"You didn't know?"

"I knew he wasn't my real brother, obviously," said Daniel. He squinted into the distance; Steel realized this was the first time he'd seen the kid without his usual wire-frame glasses. "I remember when Aja got pregnant. It was a whole big secret. Ma didn't let her out of the house, not once. Something about the shame of it all. Aja even stopped goin' to school."

"Nobody guessed?" asked Steel. Daniel's face was blank, but Steel could tell the memory was painful. Daniel shook his head. "She delivered Drew in the house, too. Mama just called a lady over from Washitaw to help deliver him- some old white lady- and that was that. She made us all promise to treat him like our brother. And we never talked about it again. After a while, I kinda forgot about it."

"Drew's eyes-"

"Yeah. I mean, I had my own ideas, about who his dad was," said Daniel, waving his hand dismissively. "But you know. It doesn't matter anyhow. Shucks, *I'm* not sure who my dad is. Grandpa's more a dad to all of us anyway." His voice hardened, but tears sprang to his eyes. He brushed them away furiously. "He's still my brother."

Steel hadn't considered it before, but if Joe Snell was truly Drew's father, he and the kid were distantly related.

"I'm going to college," Daniel said finally. He still couldn't get the tremor out off his voice, but talking about familiar subjects seemed to reassure him. "I'm takin' the SATs in August, over in Washitaw. Spanish, Math, Physics. I'm applying to Columbia."

Steel's eyebrows raised. "Why not go all the way? Get Harvard and Yale too. Or Stanford. I hear Cali's nice." He smiled, remembering when Jerry had called the Golden State a "bed of sin."

Daniel looked at him in surprise. "You're not gonna tell me it's a bad idea? That I should wait?"

It was Steel's turn to be surprised. "Why the hell would I? You got brains, kid. Wait in this town? After everything that happened?"

Daniel drew a shaky breath. He wanted to rewind the day and do it all over. He should have never have gone to Fell's Point with Travis. But the kid had insisted. He was supposed to meet Susie Murphy again. They were supposed to have been back home by five, eating Aja's delicious cooking, joking with each other, laughing...

"We're gonna be in trouble, Mr. Gray," he said. He wished he could have some of Travis's gumption. He wished his stomach would stop bubbling with anxiety. He wished he knew for sure whether Travis was okay.

"No, we aren't," Steel promised him.

"How do you know?"

Steel pulled out a recording device from his pocket. It was shiny and chrome, a new model of some equipment Daniel had never seen before. Military issue, he guessed. Steel turned it over in his palms. He rewound some of the audio; Joe Snell's voice came out clear as crystal. Clearer than crystal. Daniel's mouth hung agape. Steel snapped the audio off.

"I even have Dean Murphy's confession. I don't think these bastards are gonna talk, but anything like this gets out, it'll sink their careers. Maybe land them in prison, but that's a little optimistic. At the very least it'll keep 'em quiet, while we figure out our next move."

"My God," said Daniel, looking at Steel Gray with a new kind of respect. The man really did think of everything.

"Call it double-double insurance."

***

Aja finally came, driving Steel's pickup truck. She had been terrified the whole way to the hospital, for Travis's safety, and because getting pulled over by the police would have been a wrap for them all. She didn't have her license.

On the way there, the thought of the woman who had led them to her brothers's whereabouts kept pressing on her mind. Where had Aja met her before? And why did she seem to know so much? Lastly, Aja recalled what the woman had said, in her grating, rusty voice. *Whatever you're looking for, girlie, it's not in the Tucker house.*

Of course, she had to be talking about the Will. The Will of Fiona Tucker. That made two clues she'd been given by crazy old ladies, Aja thought wryly, remembering the message in Fiona Tucker's scrapbook. Both of them cryptic. Cryptic, yet so obvious. *Look to His cradle. Not in the house.* Whose cradle? If not the house, where? Aja couldn't remember seeing any cradles in the Tucker house, or outside it. But she also couldn't help feeling like the answer was looking her dead in the face.

She should tell Steel. Steel would help her. He'd help her look, or at least figure it out.

When she came screeching to a halt in front of the forest path, she almost jumped out of her skin at the sight of Steel and Daniel emerging from the treeline. They climbed into the car. Daniel had dried blood all over his shirt, and Steel's knuckles were torn and swollen. He'd need medical attention so they didn't get swollen.

"What did you do to them?" She asked quietly.

"Did anyone see you drive here?" Steel hedged. "I dunno. No, I don't think so."

She turned in the driver's seat to look at Daniel. He was quiet, looking out the window. "Travis is gonna be alright, Dan."

"Okay."

"We'll get you new glasses."

"Okay."

Aja's eyes filled with tears. All she wanted was a normal life with her little brothers. A normal, peaceful life. Boyd was beautiful. But the Robinsons were no longer welcome here- maybe they had never been welcome. Aja knew in her heart that they all had to leave, and leave soon. She brushed her tears away. Crying wouldn't solve anything. She'd talk to the boys when Travis was out of the hospital. Grandpa Buck, too. Aja didn't know how she'd get the money to move the family and pay for Daniel's testing and application fees. But she'd make it work. She always did.

"Do you want me to drive?" Steel asked her softly.

"No. I mean- yes. Yeah." They got out and switched places. They drove straight to the Robinson's place, dropped Daniel, then headed to the hospital. Steel saw no sign of Joe Snell or his boys. Maybe they'd gone to the Wilminac Hospital. Maybe they hadn't gone to a hospital at all.

He put his arms around Aja as they sat in the waiting room. "I'm here," he promised her. "No matter what."

"I know," she whispered. "I know."

"I love you."

"I love you, too."

***

Aja woke up in the middle of the night. She was in her own bed-alone. Steel had taken to sleeping over, but the last couple of days he'd been absent from Tucker Ranch, and he hadn't told her why. She woke up expecting to feel his strong arms around her. But she was alone.

Her eyes took some time to adjust to the darkness. This was her room, her house. The boys were sleeping downstairs- except Travis, who was still laid up in the hospital. Grandpa Buck was in his bedroom down the hall; she could hear his deep, sonorous snores. Aja eyed the clock on her dresser. 5:13 AM.

She moved as if in a trance. She put on a sweater, loose cotton pants, and her tennis shoes. She hadn't thrown them away, though Steel had told her to. The toe of one was still stained with blood.

Aja walked down the stairs, her brown hand feeling the grainy banister. She felt like she was floating on a dream. *Look to the Cradle. Not in the house. The cradle...the cradle…*

The facts were plain. They had no money anymore. Aja had slaved and pinched and saved for months-years. But Travis's hospital visit and surgery cost thousands of dollars. Money that was supposed to go towards Daniel's school, towards getting them the hell out of Boyd. Aja would have to mortgage the house to pay it off. And then she'd be trapped here for good.
The thoughts came to her in rapid succession but she felt no anxiety, no worry. She simply let them pass through her. Something

inside Aja told her everything would be alright.

Her feet carried her out the door and over the porch. She was walking to Steel's house. She wondered if he'd be there. Would he be asleep? Or would he be awake, like she was, wandering over the pastures like a ghost?

The thought of ghosts reminded Aja of the strange woman that had led them to her brothers. Lyn Thompson. The woman Steel had told her he found sitting on his property on the Fourth of July. When Aja had helped her into Steel's truck that fateful day, the woman's skin had been papery, dry and warm. Not ghostly at all. But she seemed to know things, and to Aja she had appeared horribly familiar. She realized the woman just reminded her of Fiona Tucker.

What you're looking for isn't in the house.

Aja dared not to dream anymore. It was a foolish family legend that her Grandfather had fed them. He should have known better. He shouldn't have filled her head with fantasies of riches, riches that she hadn't earned. Riches that didn't belong to her.

But Aja had nothing left but hope. Even Steel couldn't help her now, though he was always pressing her to let him pay off her debt to Joe Snell. How much money did Steel Gray have, for him to be throwing it at her like that?

Aja knew now that she'd have to swallow her pride and accept his help. She couldn't afford a debt to Joe Snell and a hospital bill like the one poor Travis was racking up during his stay at the Sacred Heart Hospital in Washitaw.

What you're looking for isn't in the house. She had to hope. The lady Fiona Tucker- who, when Aja was a young girl, would always send her Grandfather over with candy for Aja and her mother- had to have left them something. Grandpa Buck had been so sure of it. He wouldn't lie to Aja.

"Find the diary," he'd told her. "You find the diary, you get the Will."

Aja ducked under the pasture fence that separated her property and Steel's. To her immense surprise, there was a horse grazing in it.

She stood still, careful not to spook it. Her heart thrilled in excitement. She loved horses, and always had. Who owned this one? Could it be Steel's?

It was a full moon that night. Everything was awash in blue, but visible. Aja could tell it was a gray Appaloosa mare. She didn't know too much about horses, but she knew that kind was rare. The speckles on its coat were dark; possibly black. It was slender and graceful.

To Aja's surprise, a second horse emerged from the darkness of the barn to join the first. This one was heavier, with a broad, strong back and a powerful gait.

She watched them in surprise and joy. How easy would it be to saddle one up and ride away from her problems? But that was the trouble with running away, she supposed- you couldn't take the people you loved with you.

Her heart skipped as the tall, powerful form of Steel Gray emerged from the barn. He had a cowboy hat on his head, an open button-down shirt, jeans, and cowboy boots. The dusty glint of a week-old beard shimmered on his face. She watched as he fed the horses with oats from his hands, as he brushed their coats, and examined their shoes, with an expert touch. *They're his*, she realized. *He must have just bought them*.

Steel didn't talk much about his childhood in Texas, but Aja could tell he'd spent his whole life longing to relive it, regretting that he'd left. The way he'd taken to life in Boyd gave every indication. He was ready to settle down, and return to his roots.

Aja also knew that the Tucker barn had stood empty ever since John Tucker died. She'd never been inside, though her little brothers had, and so had Drew. They'd said it was neat as a pin, just a little dusty, as if someone had cleaned it a final time, long ago, then forgotten. It made her happy to see Steel using it.

Aja crept around the edge of the pasture. It seemed important that Steel not catch sight of her. She wanted to see if she could sneak past his hair-trigger senses. He didn't notice her movement; he was fixed on the beautiful horses. She smiled. She'd surprise him in the stable.

She climbed over the outer edge of the pasture fence and slipped into the stable. It was dark, but the sun was rising inch by inch and the moonlight was still strong. She surveyed it quickly. Two of the six mangers were full. There was new equipment hanging on the walls- leather saddles, rope, tack, that must have cost hundreds- if not thousands- of dollars.

A fresh saddle blanket was draped over the stall. Aja went up to it and sniffed- it didn't smell like horse at all; she guessed it was brand new. She pulled it off and wrapped it around herself. Then she sat down and waited. She picked up the sound of Steel murmuring to the horses outside.

For some strange reason, the words of an old Christmas hymn were coming into her head.

Away in a manger, no crib for a bed,
The little Lord Jesus laid down his sweet head.

Aja remembered when Drew had been small enough to rest on her stomach. Drew had been small enough to fit in a manger, too. She remembered nursing him under her Mama's supervision, swaddling him to hold in her arms when the nights got too cold. Travis had been only three years old, and fascinated with his new baby "brother". *Is he swaddled like the baby Jesus?* He'd asked. Mama had gotten a kick out of that.

Aja stared at the mangers. To think the baby Jesus had had to sleep in one of those.

Something in her head clicked into place.

"Aja?"

Steel Gray entered the stable, the budding daylight casting a halo around his golden head. He looked like he hadn't slept a wink, but he was grinning. "What are you doing here? You ruined the surprise."

Aja blinked. "Surprise?"

"Come outside, babygirl."

Still wrapped in the rather itchy saddleblanket, Aja went outside with Steel to look at the horses. They were peaceful as could be, grazing in a corner of the pasture.

"Wait here." He led the lithe Appaloosa to her, cooing and humming to it as if it were a woman. Aja's heart caught in her throat. The horse was a dream. She had long, dark lashes, a soft muzzle and a gentle nip. Aja rubbed a hand along her velvety coat, mystified. She turned to Steel, a question in her eyes.

"She's yours," he told her.

"M-mine?" Aja stammered.

"Yep."

She kept stroking the beautiful creature, trying to piece it all together. A horse like this was worth a lot of money. Then she chastised herself- why did she always have to think in terms of money? Still- this was too much. She couldn't accept this gift. Not when she had bills to pay, a brother in the hospital, and moves to make. What would she do with a horse? She said as much to Steel, who took her hands in both of his and turned her towards him.

"Aja, relax."

"Steel-"

His eyes were bright, and earnest. He looked at her seriously. "I paid Travis's hospital bills. All of them."

Aja blinked. "What?"

"These last few days I tracked down Joe Snell and I paid your debt to him, too." He said it matter-of-factly, as if he was telling her he'd bought groceries or cleaned the fridge.

"I didn't ask you- I didn't mean-" This was too much. She jerked her hands from his and stepped back. What was he playing at? Was he suddenly made of money now? Did he intend to buy her loyalty? Her love?

"Will you calm down?" He said.

"Steel, I can't do this. I can't accept these- these *gifts* - when I have nothing to give you. I don't know why you're so fixed on fixing me. This is my life- I'm responsible-"

"Stop pitying yourself for one damn second," snapped Steel, grabbing her shoulders roughly. "Who cares about that? Your brother is fine. Daniel can apply to college. You can stay in Boyd. It's alright; everything will be alright."

Aja swallowed guiltily. She had been letting her emotions run with her. Steel was right. Hang her pride for a second. He'd done an amazing thing. In the blink of an eye, he'd taken care of all her worries.

"I...Thank you," she said quietly.

Steel raised his eyes to the sky, as if praying for patience. "You're welcome."

"But," she swallowed, looking up at him through her eyelashes, in that tantalizing way she had, "Who says we want to stay in Boyd?"

Steel looked at her. "Damn you, woman."

"What?"

"Are you daft? Then obviously I'll come with you. We can move in together. Who says we have to be in Boyd?"

"What about my family?" she cried.

"What about them? They'll come too."

Aja was in disbelief. She searched his face for the inkling of a lie. But she knew better; this was Steel Gray. Steel never lied. He was talking about their future, a future she never thought she'd have with him. She had been so certain that he'd be gone from Boyd by next year, never to see her again. He'd forget all about the black girl who had fallen in love with him. He'd marry a rich white woman named Isabella- probably a foreigner- and go live his life in a chateau somewhere tropical.

Aja hadn't dared to hope that Steel would stay with her. She'd learned a long time ago that hoping too hard on anything was the main ingredient for disappointment. She wouldn't be fooled again.

Yet here he was, standing right in front of her, making all her private fantasies a reality. Aja forced herself to be calm. She still had standards. Rules for herself. She couldn't just move in with a man, even a man like Steel, without some assurances.

In a small voice, she said, "But then we'd have to be married."

"So marry me," he said immediately.

Aja was lost for words. She flung her arms around his neck; he wrapped his around her waist and lifted her up. He spun her around, happiness filling him like air in a balloon. He felt like he could fly. The words had blurted out of him, he hadn't thought about it for a second, but she had agreed. Aja would be his, at last.

He set her down and eased his mouth over hers. His tongue probed at her lips, and she opened to him like a rose.

Her soft, plump body molded against his as he deepened the kiss, bending her at the waist. Blood surged through his veins. He could feel her heartbeat thudding against his, the heaving of her generous breasts pressing against his chest. She was the most beautiful woman he had ever seen in his life; his beautiful black queen.

He wanted to keep her forever. He wanted to spend the rest of his life with her, and father her children- as many as she wanted.

They led the horses in and then walked back to his house; it was closer, and they both were desperate to consummate their engagement.

When they got to the house, Steel bent and lifted Aja over the mantelpiece, bridal style. He couldn't wait to tear her clothes off. He dumped her in the soft couch and peeled them off. She wasn't wearing any underwear, thank god. Her generous breasts splayed over her stomach- Steel could have sworn they had gotten more full. He didn't pause to ask; he mauled them with his hands and took each blackberry-colored nipple in his mouth, suckling and lapping like his life depended on it. His fingers dipped to her creamy moistness below, the deep, soft passage that would take the full length of him soon without complaint. Aja mewled and moaned under his ministrations, her pussy gushing over his fingers, wanting him to fill her with something larger.

But of course he took a minute to taste her throbbing wetness, lapping at her folds until the fire built inside her, roaring with heat until it exploded in a shower of stars. Aja couldn't hold back her screams of pleasure as Steel made love to her with his long tongue, plowing her secret hole until she begged for more release.

Then his cock was out, and he was guiding it towards her mouth.

"Open up, beautiful," he murmured, his tumescent pole pushing past her lips into a heavenly, drenching heat. As much as Steel loved the feeling of stretching out Aja's tight little pussy, he loved delving into her throat too. She had learned how to suck him off just the way he liked. Today he let her do the work. She drooled and gagged but took him all in as she always did, loving the feeling of his enormous cock wedged inside her throat. She wanted to feel him cum filling her belly again. She wanted to be his. Aja sucked and gagged and drooled all over his cock until the need in her was almost as great as his. Unconsciously one hand went to her pussy, playing with its wet folds. She found the nub of her desire and stroked it.

The sight of Aja touching herself as he fucked her mouth made Steel wild with desire. He couldn't bear it; Steel threw back his head and exploded in her greedy mouth, ropes of cum battering Aja's throat. He came so much it filled her mouth and spurted out over her lips. Aja drank every drop, like the good girl she was. The sight of her brown and plump body poised and ready to serve his white cock drove him to the brink again. He turned her over and released the power in his big body, spearing her with his dick until she moaned with pure pleasure and her pussy flooded around him. But he wasn't in a rough mood tonight. He plowed her slowly, each stroke hard and deliberate. The rhythm consumed them. Aja gasped at how deep he thrusted; she felt him all the way in her chest. His invading cock stretched the walls of her pussy to accommodate his girth. She was all too willing, set aflame by bursts of ecstasy that flared inside her again and again. His need became her own. He was making her his. She belonged to him now, and she would serve his dick for as long as he wanted, just as his dick would service her. Aja surrendered to his incessant thrusts completely, letting him ride her into the heights of pleasure.

Steel watched Aja's ass slapping against his thighs. He wondered how many ways he could take her like this. He'd never get tired of his black queen. He'd never get tired of her pussy, so tight he felt he was digging it out with every thrust. Aja always came when she had her ass in the air like that, and this time was no exception.

Every inch she took inside of her, every sound she made fed an animal desire inside Steel. He wanted to claim her. She was his, and his alone. He wanted her like this always. He'd keep her in his bed, pleasuring her, using her when his own pleasure needed attending to.

Aja looked up at Steel and knew she wanted to be his woman

forever. She had found a real man in him, someone who would love her and treat her right. She desired him physically. Her body craved the release that only his could offer. And when he drove into her, she felt him touch the very corners of her soul before she came, shaking, to blissful reality again.

They exploded with each other in a blaze of rapture, Steel unleashing jets of cum into her needy passage. Aja was filled to overflowing, both with his seed and with her emotions.
Finally they held each other, riding out the last waves of pleasure together in the comforting harbor of each other's arms.

"Aja," said Steel finally, when they were quiet at last. His fingertips were tracing the length of her spine, light as a kiss.

"Mmm?" She replied. Her face was buried in his chest; she was stroking the soft golden curls there too.

"I know about Drew. I know he's your son."

Aja froze, then breathed deeply. One breath, in and out. She sighed.

"I guess it's time...It's time you knew. I expected that you'd figure it out."

"Yeah."

"Do you care?" Her voice was small and tentative.

He raised her up to look at him. The look on his face was both incredulous and amused.

"You think I'd care about something like that?"

She looked at him seriously. Her soft brown eyes were wide.

"No. No, you wouldn't," she said finally.

"Exactly. Besides, at this point he feels like my kid too. They all do."

Aja flung her arms around his neck again. He kissed her soft mouth again, his cock already stiffening for another round between them. Aja drove him crazy. She made him happy and crazy all at once. How did she do that?

Aja couldn't express what these words meant to her; how he'd just made her the happiest woman in the world. Her whole life she'd been waiting to hear a man say that. She'd been waiting for someone to share her life with, with all it's trials and inconsistencies. And Steel Gray had braved them all with her, the worst and the very best. He wanted to marry her and he wanted to share her life. What more could she possibly want?

CHAPTER SEVEN

...WILL BE BROUGHT TO THE LIGHT

Joe Snell clutched the rag to his nose, doing his best to take shallow breaths. Ever since his last run-in with Steel Gray he hadn't been able to breathe properly- another tally on the long list of damages. Just thinking about that day made his blood boil over, but it wouldn't do to slip up now, when so much relied on him keeping calm.

The gasoline splashed all over his shoes. "Fuck," he hissed. He had about ten minutes to complete this job, then he'd be out the basement door, in his car and away from here before anyone could ever know. It was a calculated endeavor, one he'd been planning for the past two weeks as soon as he'd gotten clear of the hospital.

Joe continued up the stairs quietly, a trail of gas sloshing behind him. The container was getting lighter and lighter, which was good because he wasn't as strong as he used to be. He doused the curtains downstairs, the sofa, leaving a nice trail to the stairs. The smell was overpowering.

The damage Steel had dealt had been mostly to Joe's face and ribcage. What enraged Joe the

most was that even as he'd laid
under Steel absorbing the man's
furious blows, he could tell the big
Texan had been holding back. If
he had wanted to kill Joe, he
would have. He could have.

The damage had been a broken
nose, broken jaw, contusions on
his cheeks, forehead, and chin,
two missing teeth, a split lip, and
a damaged eardrum. Joe still
couldn't breathe properly. He still
had to keep a mostly liquid diet,
and his hearing was damaged-
permanently, the doctor had said.
Joe might have to get a hearing
aid.

Ironically, that was what sank Joe
Snell's career for good. Already
the regional superintendent had
called for him to be put under

investigation- it seemed Daniel Robinson, the uppity brat, had filed an anonymous report. Joe knew because Daniel had told him as much himself- emboldened by the Gray bastard, no doubt. The report was an incriminating piece of work, to say the least. He had wondered how on earth the kid had dug it all up. But even if Joe Snell put his connections to good use and cleared the charges- which he was sure he could have done- the loss of his hearing meant he was no longer fit to serve. A policeman needed all his faculties working. Not even Joe Snell could get around that.

Joe pushed the thought out of his mind. He had bigger things to think about right now- like getting out of this house without anyone seeing him. Like the gasoline canister in his hand, the lighter in his pocket, and the fact that at any moment, the people sleeping upstairs could hear him.

Aja was one of these people. Aja Robinson. That black bitch. He had loved her. He had wanted to make her love him. Serve him. There had even been a time- back when Drew was still a little blue-eyed toddler- when Joe had been this close to getting her to marry him. She had refused then, and kept refusing for twelve years, no matter how many promises he made, no matter how much money and presents he put at her feet. She was a stubborn cuss, but Joe was so sure she would turn around eventually.

After he had ravished her that fateful night- with the help of Pat Tucker- he'd been sure she'd see reason and agree to be his woman.

Many a night Joe had lain awake and thought about what he'd done. He felt no remorse, of course. Just a seething rage. The look on Aja's face when he'd finished! As if she had a right to look that way! As if he hadn't honored her, as if he hadn't put it all on the line for her. In the years since he'd tried to do better by her, be sweet, to lure her back to his side; she hadn't deserved the good treatment, but he'd done it. Still, it hadn't worked.

He'd been a fool. But he'd have the last laugh.

Joe finished his work, sloshing the last few drops in the doorway. He pulled out his lighter and struck it.

It didn't catch.

He stared. *You've got to be joking.* He thumbed it furiously, but the spark fizzled weakly and died. He shook it; there was plenty of liquid in the chamber. The thing was just dead.

"Need some help, honey?"

The voice sounded like nails rattling in a bucket, like stones rolling down a mountain. Joe Snell jumped out of his skin. He turned face to face with a woman he thought he'd never see again. Lyn Thompson. Or, as she had once been called, Lynette Murphy.

***

6 HOURS EARLIER

It was late in the night, or early in the morning- depending on how you looked at it- and Steel was intertwined with the woman he loved, his hands resting on her generous ass, reflecting. They had spent most of the past couple days out riding. The horses were like ghosts beneath them. They were gentle creatures, and strong. Aja hadn't ridden a horse in years, but Dream was such an easy and forgiving creature that soon it was all coming back. Steel had named his Wanderer. Like Dream, Wanderer had taken to Steel immediately. They spent all day on horseback, ambling through the rolling hills of Boyd, visiting every farm they crossed. Steel had to admit he liked seeing Aja on horseback. But he also liked the feeling of the big animal beneath his thighs. It reminded him of his youth herding cattle through the Texas prairie.

"You were a real cowboy, huh?" Aja had teased.

"Sure was," Steel said, exaggerating his Texas drawl. Aja laughed, as he knew she would.

"You ever miss it?"
"All the time. I've been thinking of going back. "

"I'm coming with you."

"Of course you are."

Steel had been doing his homework. He had his eye on a ranch in Texas, a little bit smaller than Boyd. He'd put out the notice, secretly, through his connections, that black farmers across the state could purchase the land or cheap. That way the boys would never have to feel out of place again. Aja could, for the first time, be with her people.

Even if he never picked up herding again, he'd have something to leave for his children, and Aja's brothers, for the rest of their lives.

He thought about that as he lay in Aja's bed, her soft body twined around him. He stroked her hair, thinking. It was all working out.

They would be happy. He drifted off to sleep.

***

Aja woke an hour later to the sight of her grandfather's face, drawn with concern. He was clutching something to his chest.

"Wake up, girl. Wake up."

"Huh?" It was dark outside. Her grandfather was never up this late. Something was wrong.

Grandpa Buck put a finger to his lips. "Shush, now. Git up. Don't wake up your man."

Aja slid out of bed, careful not to touch Steel. He gave a little snore.

"What's wrong?" she whispered. Her grandfather led her out of the room and closed the door. His voice was low and urgent.

"I found it." He reached into his jacket pocket and pulled out a book. It was leather-bound, with gold leaf pages. Aja took it and flipped it open. The spidery handwriting was unmistakable. This was Fiona Tucker's diary.

"How?" Aja said. She couldn't believe it.

"It was in your Grandma Sara's old quarters," said Grandpa Buck. "The last place anyone would look. The old closet."

"You were in the house? You broke in?"

"I found it, didn't I?" the old man said defensively. "Here." He flipped through to the end of the book. Aja strained to read the writing in the dim light.

The Lord is forgiving. I have left my last requests in a place few would think to look, where Sara and I would play as children. In the cradle of our Lord Jesus Christ, where he lay humbly as a baby when all men had turned him away. It is to the Lord I look for deliverance and forgiveness.
 My father's evil has left a poison legacy on this family. I am as guilty as the rest of my blood, for the abuses inflicted on this woman, and on the Robinson family.

Here I shall write an account of what happened between our families.

Sara Smith, as she was then called, was given to the Tucker family as a little girl. They purchased her for fifteen dollars, though I could find no receipt of her purchase amongst my father's belongings. She was not paid; to put it plainly, she was a slave. In those times no one questioned her presence. My father John Tucker and my mother Lydia Tucker kept her a secret. I regret to say that Sarah endured all manner of abuse from my father. He kept her as a bedmate when she was not yet fourteen, a fact that drove my mother, in turn, to beat her when my father was not around. For many years she suffered, and I, of an age with Sara, was ignorant to many of these abuses. My father allowed his friends to use her when they came to visit. She also bore a child for my father, to my recollection. They were torn from her breast and spirited away in the night. The Good Lord in his mercy only knows what happened to the child. I believe it was a boy. Sarah never saw him again.

When Sara was eighteen we hired a gardener, one Buck Robinson, who in the years since Sara's passing has become a close friend of mine. Sara and Mr. Robinson fell in love. I do not doubt that if my father had discovered this, he would have killed them both. It was through Mr. Robinson's efforts, and with small help from myself, that Sara Smith was rescued from our family's clutches. She and Mr. Robinson soon married. But I regret to say that would not be the last time the Robinsons were preyed upon by my family.

I learned only recently that the grandchild of Sara Robinson, by name of Aja Robinson, was the victim of a violent sexual act perpetrated by my brother Patrick Tucker and the Sheriff of Boyd County, Joe Snell (to my understanding, Joe Snell is descended from one of my father's bastards as well). Miss Robinson was then ostracized by the people of Boyd County, and has been the target of further abuses from Mr. Snell.

My last request is an effort to put an end to this evil legacy of the Tucker family. I die with only two living relatives. One is my nephew, Carson Tucker. The other is a distant cousin of mine, by name of Steel Edward Gray, whose details I have given to Carson so the two may be in contact. Carson will inherit only a small fraction of the Tucker fortune. Steel will inherit nothing. Finally, I shall say for the record that my research has revealed that the Tucker fortune did not originate in Boyd, but in Plum Tree, South Carolina. My great-grandfather owned a large cotton plantation with over a hundred slaves. The monies from this formed the foundation of the Tucker fortune. As of today we are still the owners of this land, drawing rent from tenants monthly.

This poisoned lineage ends with me. I have left the crucial details in my Will, which shall be discovered by the right person when it is time. I only ask for forgiveness from the Robinson family, and deliverance for myself.

-Fiona Mae Tucker

Aja read the entry again and again, her mind reeling. Here it was. Concrete proof. Her grandfather hadn't been crazy, there *was* a will left for the Robinson family.

Her eyes filled with tears. What her grandmother had gone through! Seeing her son torn away, the rape, the abuse, the generational suffering. Even seeing her own name in print was shocking. Memories from that night flooded her mind. Patrick Tucker- Carson's father- standing over Aja, waiting his turn...the sweat, the blood. Bile rose in Aja's throat; she clenched her thighs together and slammed the journal shut.

"How did you find this?" she whispered hoarsely.

"Ah remembered," Grandpa Buck said miserably. "She'd tol' me where it was. Before she died. Ah just forgot...forgot that she'd told me." His own eyes were bright with tears.

"It's alright," Aja said, hugging him. She remembered when her

Grandpa had seemed like the strongest man in the world, so tall and muscular. He'd had a tongue as sharp as the devil's, and a temper to match. No one had messed with Buck Robinson. Now he was weak and shrunken with age. His mind was fraying at the edges.

"The Will," Grandpa Buck said, grabbing her arm suddenly. "She left clues."

"I know," Aja told him. Excitement coursed through her veins, like fire over gasoline. "I think I finally figured it out."

***

Aja climbed back into bed and fell asleep immediately, her mind dark as the night outside. She slept.

***

Steel Gray was having a
nightmare. It was the usual kind
he had. He was in uniform,
sweating under his fatigues, the
grease in his hair sealing the
helmet to his head like glue. He
had to be quiet- quiet as a rabbit.
No one could see him.

His breath came heavily- fear. He
was afraid. The red dust of
Afghanistan was swirling all
around him, choking him. He had
seen enough fucking dust, that
was all there was in this damned
country- dust. Dust and fear and
carnage. He was sick of it. He
wanted to go home.

He realized what building he was
entering, and his mind rebelled.

He did not like this part of the dream. He didn't want to relive it again.

Still, he walked, denied the relief of waking up. His dream self crossed the shattered doorframe of the mud house. He heard the child's crying before he saw it. His stomach twisted preemptively.

"No, no," Steel said through clenched teeth, but his dream body moved forward. There was Major Green, fatigues around his feet- and the little girl's headscarf was pulled up around her face. Hiding her from the shame.

Steel's temper flared. He was angry. He was the angriest he'd ever been in his life, the rage bursting in him like a bubble of hot poison. He raised his rifle-

"Steel! Steel!"

It was Aja, shaking him awake. He had been twisting violently in her bed. He sat up, disoriented, shaking the lingering effects of the dream from his head. Her face was framed in red light. That was the first thing that occured to him. The second was the smell.

Smoke.

He was instantly awake.

"Baby? Baby, what's wrong?"

Aja looked frantic, terrified. She was covered in sweat.

"Steel!" She sobbed, still shaking him. "The house is on fire!"

He was on his feet in seconds, his training taking over. "Where are the boys?"

"Outside. They got out the window. But Steel-"

"And your grandfather?"

Aja moaned in despair. "I don't know."

"Hold on to me."

The heat when he opened the door was overpowering. It was in the kitchen, on the bottom floor, and to Steel's horror, tongues of orange flame were licking up the stairs. The boys' window was on the second floor- they must have jumped.

"Let's go out their window, then."

"The documents- their birth certificates-"

Steel ignored her, seizing her arm and dragging her to Daniel's room forcefully. There wasn't time to stand and dither. He pushed her in front of the window, which was small,but which would fit Aja- he wasn't so sure about himself.

He shut the door of the room, dragging the curtains off the window and stuffing them under the door.

"Jump," he said.

"It's-" Aja swallowed, looking at him. "What about you?"

"JUMP!" Steel roared, shoving at her back. It was a twenty foot drop. She barely fit through the window. Aja could hear Daniel and Drew calling to her from below, their voices thin and tinny over the roaring in her ears. Steel was a furious tower behind her, barricading against her fear. If she didn't jump, he might kill her before the fire did.

She hit the ground rolling, as he'd instructed her to do. Smoke was pouring in through the doorframe; had the fire reached the second floor?

He eyed the window. It was too small. He had to make it wider, somehow, or he'd die. Painfully.

The frame was only wood and drywall- hardwood, he thought

grimly. This house was old, after all.

His eyes scanned the room. Daniel and Travis shared this room. The bunk bed was wrought iron, but he couldn't lift it. Posters on the wall. A basketball. A bookshelf. Baseball bat- but that was aluminum, not strong enough.

His eyes settled on a baseball bat with resignation. It would have to do. But in his gut, he knew it wouldn't be enough. He was going to die. Here, of all places. After all he had lived through- this was it. The room steadily filled with smoke. A few more minutes and it would be hard to breathe. He'd lose oxygen, wouldn't be able to think-

The door banged open, smoke pouring into the room. It was Drew Robinson. The boy was coughing harshly, his blue eyes streaming. The tips of his shirt were singed. He was holding his shirt to his nose. In his left hand he held an axe. The kind for splitting wood.

"Drew?!" Steel exclaimed in disbelief. The boy had come back in the house- somehow, insanely. "Are you crazy?"

"S-shut up!" Drew coughed, dropping the hatchet at his feet. "Hurry!"

"How the hell-"

It was his turn to get yelled at. "Get the window!" the boy screamed.

Steel wasted no time. He tore into the window frame with all his strength, chips flying, his eyes bright with determination. The axe was a blur in his hands. Adrenaline coursed through his body. It took him only a minute. Drew was wide enough to fit through but he refused to jump until Steel was finished.

The axe flew for a final time. Panting, Steel turned to the boy, who was wheezing on the floor. His nose was stuffed in the shirt, and he was struggling to breathe. Drew turned desperate eyes to him.

In the distance, sirens.

***

Buck Robinson avoided mirrors. Since he'd hit his sixties, he'd started to hate the damn things. He supposed it was vanity- he'd been a handsome young guy, that was sure. Tall and strong and capable. When old age started to come down on him, the sight of his liver spots, wrinkles, shaking hands and yellow nails were horrifying. They made him recoil in disgust. He was repulsed by his own reflection; by the weak thing he had become.

And he'd never admit it either, but Buck Robinson was afraid of death.

Not that death was a stranger to him. It was precisely because he'd been so familiar with it that he feared it. To hell with what anyone said. You didn't grow numb to death. You just pushed the fear away.

As Buck moved towards the Tucker barn, something made him stop. He listened. It was the sound of sirens, coming on the wind like a wolf's howl. Buck spun around; smoke was rising from the place over the hill. Thick, black smoke- the kind that meant burning houses. He sniffed, his eyes suddenly watering.

Was it the Robinson house? With Aja and the boys?

The thought came to him from a distant place. It was too surreal- *surreal*- a word Daniel, his grandson, had taught him. Feeling emotionless, he turned around and started to limp towards the sirens. Then he paused.

Heated voices came from the porch of the Tucker House. Buck heard them and ducked behind a hydrangea bush. Maybe it was Aja and Steel- maybe the boys were with them.

It was not Aja and it was not Steel. It was actually Lyn Thompson, a woman Buck had thought he'd never see again, and Joe Snell. The Sheriff.

Snell was clutching onto the woman's arms with a deathly grip. Her hands were ziptied. She was hurling all kinds of abuses at him. He backhanded her viciously across the face. She fell in a heap to the ground, her white hair a frazzled halo. Buck watched in astonishment as Joe dragged the woman's crumpled body inside the foyer, and shut the door on her.

The tall man then jogged down the steps to his car, which was hidden in a clump of bushes. Buck stood frozen in place, watching it all unfold like a horrible sick movie. Joe hauled a container of gasoline behind him. He doused the porch liberally, then set the canister down and jogged back to his car again. This time he returned with strips of plywood and a clear plastic bag full of nails. He held the hammer between his teeth.

Buck's breath was ragged. He had to do something. But only a stone's throw away his house was on fire- with his family inside it. He had to get over that pasture fence to rescue them, Lyn Thompson be damned…

Joe Snell began hammering the door shut. Buck shuddered. He wished he were thirty years younger, but he wasn't.

He could hear the Thompson woman screaming inside. *Jesus Christ Almighty*. He needed a distraction.

"Hey, you donkey-head motherfucker!" Buck bellowed.

Joe couldn't hear him. He didn't even turn around. *Bang bang bang* went the hammer.

Buck hollered and waved, but the man didn't move. So Buck limped to the Sheriff's car, keeping low behind the bushes. He hoped the old bastard was too distracted to turn around. The key was still in the engine; Snell had clearly organized it to make a clean escape. Buck didn't go for the key immediately. He opened the glove compartment first. Surely a man like Joe Snell had a spare gun in his car.

Buck was disappointed; rummaging through, he found there was nothing in there but empty cigarette boxes. Then his fingertips hit something cold and metallic. Buck froze. He felt for the handle. He carefully withdrew a long Bowie knife. The engraving on the blade flashed unmistakably: *John Augustus Tucker.*

Sometimes, life itself could be a mirror. Things reflecting in endless sequence. It had been so many years since Buck Robinson had held the knife that had made him famous West of the Mississippi, before he'd had to run for his life and settle down in Boyd, Virginia. Some men had preferred

Joe Snell hammered the last nail in, the screams of Lyn Thompson like a whine in his ears. He climbed off the porch. The smell of gasoline was already giving him a headache. He was struggling for breath already, damn it. Joe realized that he'd wasted time going through the Robinson house- one didn't need to be *too* thorough to start a fire.

The Tucker House was old and strong, and almost entirely made of wood. Over the last hundred years or so it had been remodeled but once. Since his last visit, Steel Gray had set up plants on the porch in pots and boxes, clearly striving for a cozy, welcoming feel. They did add to the appeal of the old house. Oh well. Snell splashed some gasoline on the flowers too.

He had to be quick. Once the fire department quenched the building next door, no doubt they'd come over the pasture to check on the neighbors too. Snell didn't intend to be around when they did.

Lyn Thompson had quit her racket, finally. Perhaps the cow was trying for another escape route in the house. Joe wondered if he should have just shot her, damn the risk of being heard. The hag had caused no end of trouble for him ever since she popped up in Boyd five years ago. Always poking her nose where it didn't belong. The only thing keeping her at bay was the threat of Joe revealing exactly who she was to the good people of Boyd; but lately she'd been getting bolder. Who cared about some crime an old lady had committed over thirty years ago? It wasn't like she'd killed anybody. Some people probably considered shooting the knees out of brutish John Tucker heroic.

Lost in his thoughts, and fumbling for his lighter, Joe didn't notice Buck Robinson until he felt the cold, sharp blade pressing up against his kidneys.

"Ah don't need a reason," whispered Robinson. Joe went perfectly still.

"I don't believe this," Joe whispered. "You old bastard."

"Put ya hands behind ya head," said the old man. There was a steel edge in his voice that Joe wasn't expecting. "Real slow, now. Don't try no shit with me."

"Killing me isn't going to- ouch!"

Joe felt a rivulet of blood running down his back, soaking into his waistband. Did he want to risk disarming the old geezer?

He did. Joe spun quickly, stepping back from the old man and John Tucker's bowie knife. He reached for a gun at his waist that wasn't there; with dawning horror, he remembered he'd given it up when they took his badge. And Robinson, with a tenacious instinct that he'd thought had been buried long ago by time, moved fast.

The knife sliced through Joe's shirt in a wicked red line. The younger man hollered and jumped, his feet slipping in the slick gasoline he'd poured himself. Down he went, with Buck Robinson following. Buck remembered that this was the man that had shamed his granddaughter, that had terrorized his grandsons, that had threatened the family into silence for years. That put his grandson Travis in the hospital. And putting two and two together, he figured that Snell was likely responsible for the blaze over the pasture- the house he'd bought with Sara all those years ago. The house that she'd never got to enjoy.

Red clouded his vision. Buck roared and fell upon the younger man. Joe scrambled back away from the blade, crying out. He realized he was afraid, very desperately afraid. There was no other way this could end. He fumbled in his pocket for the lighter.

The two men rolled against each other. They were covered in gasoline and blood. It stung Joe's wounds. Joe was sobbing for breath, holding Robinson's arms away from him. The look in the old black man's eyes wasn't human. He had the knife an inch away from Joe's eye, driving the point with all the strength left in him towards its bloody conclusion.

Joe Snell snapped the zippo lighter open, and dropped it.

***

Aja held Drew for a long time, her whole body shaking. The boy kept trying to pull out of her grip- she held him fast, crying and crying, until the medics had to physically restrain her so they could take him into the Ambulance. According to the EMTs, they all needed to be treated for oxygen deprivation. Steel refused, and so did Aja, but Drew, who was the worst of them all, had no choice. Aja would have forced him to do it even if he'd refused. She seemed incapable of letting him out of her sight.

Daniel looked pale and frightened when they put the mask over his face. It wasn't two minutes before he pulled it off, and strode over to Aja.

"I wasn't watching him," he said miserably. "He got out of my sight- I'm so sorry- he could have- he almost-"

Aja flung her arms around her oldest brother's neck and cried harder. Steel hung back. He had never seen her so hysterical; he wanted to offer words of comfort, say something. Inside he just felt dead. They still didn't know where Grandpa Buck was.

The whole story of Steel's impossible rescue was soon revealed. Apparently, when Drew realized that Steel couldn't fit through the window, he had doubled out back to the shed. Daniel had been busy on the phone directing the fire department. Drew had stuck Grandpa Buck's axe through his belt and scaled the old bottle tree that scraped the side of the house. Then he'd jumped in through the small bathroom window on the second floor-which, by some miracle of chance, someone had left open.

It was a feat of astonishing bravery and nerve, one that Drew would remember- and be remembered by- for the rest of his life.

 If someone had closed the window. If she had had the bottle tree's branches cut like she'd kept wishing to these last few months. If the shed had been locked. If Drew hadn't been strong enough to carry the axe. If the fire had been a moment quicker. If Steel had been a moment slower. All these impossible twists of fortune led to Aja's son and lover still being alive and in front of her. She fell to her knees and thanked God.

Steel went to her at last, his arms wrapping around her. "Drew-"

"He saved your life."

"He did. I'm so grateful. I- I don't know what to say."

Aja turned her face towards his and kissed him.

"Steel," said Daniel urgently, interrupting them.

"Huh?"

The boy's alarmed gaze was directed over the hill, towards the Tucker House. They followed it to the thin trail of gray smoke rising and disappearing in the shadow of the mountain.

"Oh," Steel said.

"Oh, my god," said Aja.

***

Lyn Thompson had, in fact, found an exit. Still bleary from Joe's blow to her temple, it had taken her a few minutes to calm down and use her head, but she found it. She'd heard the two men arguing, then watched them grapple on the porch through the window. Her only thought was to get the hell away as fast as possible and call for help. She'd sawed off the zipties binding her hands with a knife from the kitchen. The escape she chose was through the parlor window on the other side of the house, which she smashed with the urn of John Tucker himself. Somehow she found the strength to lift that thing and fling it. It had been messy- brown dust flew everywhere- but once the pane shattered, she climbed out and was free.

The twisted screams of Buck Robinson were what pulled her back from her determined course to get as far away from the house as possible. She had heard his voice from behind the door- she'd recognize it anywhere. Buck had been a friend to Lyn for a long time, before Lynnette was Lyn Thompson, when she was young and still living in Boyd. It was she who had told Buck of Sara Smith's existence, and it was she who had helped them escape.

To return the favor, Buck had helped her re-settle in Boyd, once the cloud surrounding her name had been lifted. He'd helped her build her house deep in the

Shenandoah, where no one ever bothered her again.

She owed him.

This was what Lyn thought as she doubled around to the front of the house, as fast as her old legs could go. She realized immediately that she was too late. The sight and smoke was horrible; the two men were writhing on the porch, engulfed in a blazing inferno. One of them launched himself onto the grass, rolling, rolling, to douse the fire on his clothes. There was nothing she could do but stand, horrified, and look on. The man's hair was a pillar of flame. His screams were not human.

The fire on the porch caught the doorframe, spreading quickly over the mantelpiece, on the windows, licking up the sides of the house. The second body was motionless, burning sluggishly. And soon the moving man fell to the ground, and was perfectly still.

Lyn heard shouts from over the hill. She froze, her old heart thumping in her chest.

If she stayed, they could accuse her. They would think she did it. She was the crazy old mountain lady, after all. The woman who had shot the knees out of John Tucker. The woman with a reputation.

If she left, no one would know what happened. She'd be free to die in peace and anonymity- like she had always wanted. But Buck Robinson's family would want answers. Didn't she owe them that?

Her mind made up, Lyn hobbled to the barn, ducking under the pasture fence. Dream and Wanderer, the horses Steel had bought a few days ago, were frightened by the smell of the fire; their ears flicked frantically, pawing at the hay.

She moved straight past them, to the end of the rows of mangers. Fiona Tucker had been about as sharp as a marble, but the woman had had a good heart. Lyn had been in and out of the Tucker house numerous times since Fiona's death. The two had been good friends, ever since John Tucker died. Oh yes, Lyn Thompson knew about the journal and the scrapbook clues, and figuring out what they meant had been about as hard as spitting.

But Lyn had left it all alone- she was a curious old hag, she'd admit that any day. And she observed things most people didn't. But she also liked people to figure things out for themselves. Buck Robinson had kept harassing her to tell him. For months, she'd evaded his questions. But he'd gotten more insistent, so finally, so he'd leave her alone, she told him about the diary's location. Little did she know it would all go south so damn quickly!

The will was inside the manger, wrapped in three ziploc bags, and inside a wooden case. Lyn didn't have to open it to know the contents- her signature was on it. She'd been present when it was signed, as the witness. It deeded the house and land in Boyd to Carson Tucker, but the vast majority of the Tucker Fortune- around two million in total- would be put in the hands of the eldest Robinson child, Aja.

By the time she made her way out of the barn, the Steel Gray fellow had appeared. He stood far back from the house, away from the soaring flames. Covered in soot, his face was dark and ragged. Lyn was surprised to even see him alive- but then again, she didn't put anything past the big Texan. Steel had two fists locked in his hair; he stared at the burning old house in dismay. Lyn swallowed.

Buck Robinson's body lay a few yards away from the house. Steel hadn't seen it yet.

"Mr. Gray," she called, walking over.

"Lyn-?" He turned haunted eyes to her. "I don't believe this."

Lyn licked her lips. "It was Joe. He set the one by the Robinson place."

"So where the hell were you? Why didn't you call for help?"

"He had me," she snapped. "I thought I could talk the bastard out of it. But he hogtied me and made me watch when he did it. Then he dragged me over here."

"Jesus Christ."

Lyn glanced around. She could see Buck's granddaughter coming up the hill.

"God Almighty. Steel. Don't let her over here."

"What-why?"

Lyn pointed to the remains of poor old Buck Robinson. At first Steel didn't understand. But Lyn pushed him towards Aja. "Don't let her see!"

The old woman watched the rest of it unfold. The fire department only had to drive a little ways to get the second burning house under control. Steel held Aja fiercely throughout it all. Lyn watched him explain what had happened. She'd give the rest of the details later- how Buck had fought, what Joe had done. But for now Aja just had to hear the one, most important fact that brought this horrible day to its end: her grandfather was dead.

Lyn Thompson still held the box containing Fiona's will. There would be time enough for that. With a heavy heart, she watched Aja Robinson sink to her knees, the young woman's wails echoing above and beyond the cold blue mountains.

CHAPTER EIGHT
HAPPY AFTER ALL

ONE YEAR LATER

"Hey!" Steel laughed, pulling the horse up next to Aja. She was standing outside their house, clamping a straw hat on her head against the wind. It had been sunny all morning, but on the Texas prairie the weather could turn in the blink of an eye. Dark clouds were already rolling in from the distance, pregnant with rain.

Aja looked up at him with a grin. "When you gonna stop muckin' around out there and come inside?"

Steel dismounted. "As soon as I get Wanderer out of this. Give me a minute."

Aja watched him ride off, feeling a pang of nostalgia. She missed riding her own horse, Dream. She was glad they'd gotten the beautiful creatures to Texas after all.

Steel jogged back to the house. Despite the incoming rain- or perhaps because of it- it was so hot his shirt was sucked against his back by the sweat. He wished it were sunnier- then he and Aja could have headed down to the watering hole with the horses and had a swim.

The first thing that greeted him when he stomped inside were Travis and Drew, locked into some sports game on the Television. School was out for summer, and Aja was hard-pressed to get the two of them focused on anything else.

Still, she admitted to herself with a smile, the boys had taken to life in Texas easier than she'd thought. Travis was involved in a local all-African American dance crew. In August he'd be traveling to a competition in Atlanta. He'd bounced back from his injury so quickly, and in the past year he'd blossomed from a surly teen into a smart and capable boy.

Drew was still bound at the hip to Steel, and when he wasn't with Travis he was right in the middle of the cattle drivers, hooting and hollering with the best of them. Steel had to admit he'd never seen a kid so good with horses. It was no surprise that Drew had become a favorite among the local ranchers, who seemed to have collectively adopted him into the fold.

It had been a while since any of them had seen Daniel. The oldest Robinson brother was at Stanford now, heavily involved in their bioengineering program. One of the research schools had hired him as an intern for the summer.

Aja grinned when Steel came inside. He hung up his hat and peeled the damp shirt from his muscled body. He smelled musky and heavy, like a man should. He'd cut his hair back to shoulder-length. The curls were cloudy and big from the humidity. His blue eyes danced, bright with happiness.

"Everything okay?" Aja asked.

"Yep. Nathaniel's got the cattle all corralled in for the storm. Everything taken care of."

"Then come here."

Aja led him upstairs to their bedroom. As if reading her mind, Steel rinsed off then drew a bath for the both of them, filling it with a bottle of Aja's delicious-smelling handmade bubble bath. Since her pregnancy Aja had looked for ways to keep herself occupied. She found a hobby in making beauty products, using some herblore Grandpa Buck had taught her and Steel's green thumb to supply ingredients.

The water came from a hot springs nearby. Steel hoisted his body in the massive porcelain tub, sighing with pleasure. He watched Aja undress. Pregnancy suited her body, making her soft and warm all over. Her breasts had swelled, their blackberry colored nipples fitting perfectly inside his mouth. The weight she'd put on only enhanced her curves, with none more pronounced than the rich swell of her belly. Steel could hardly believe she was his woman. His child was growing inside her fertile womb, and his seed had put it there. Several times he had tried to guess when they might have conceived. But it was hard to tell. Since moving to Texas they had been so relieved to put Boyd behind them they'd hardly left the bed, taking delight in each other's arms as much as they delighted in their new life together.

Aja's dark skin highlighted his bronze tan as she climbed carefully into the tub. Steel fit her easily in front of him, his hands rising to cup her large breasts. He thumbed her nipples idly.

"So, Aja Gray," he murmured, his lips brushing her ear. "How do you feel today?"

Aja smiled. Steel asked her that question every morning.

"I don't know. Alright, I guess. I'm a little tired."

"Mmm," said Steel. He sighed. "I have some news."

Aja sat up a little. "What's up?"

"I gotta go to Elaine's tomorrow. There's a big cattle sale and inspection. Might take two days, so I'll have to overnight."

Aja felt cold. Elaine Jemson was a blonde, blue-eyed country belle with a hefty bosom and an even bigger behind. She liked ranching just as much as Steel did, and was very good at it. She also liked flirting with other people's husbands. She was good at that as well. Aja had caught the woman eyeing Steel before in *that way*, making every excuse to touch him. The woman managed to turn into a total klutz when Steel was around. When she wasn't tripping over everything she was fussing and preening and bending over like a pigeon. Aja had tried to befriend the woman, but it was clear Elaine's interest in the Gray family centered around one person only.

Aja wasn't sure that Steel didn't like the attention, either. He was a man, after all, and Elaine was very beautiful. Besides, with Aja's pregnancy advancing, maybe he wanted to look for pleasure somewhere else. Handsome as he was, he was certainly capable of having any woman in the tightly-knit Texas community, whether they were married or not.

"I see," Aja said shortly.

Steel was privately amused at her tone. She was clearly jealous, but too proud to show it. He squeezed her against him hard, making her squeal. His teeth nipped her ear.

"Jealous?" he whispered, feeling her shiver beneath him. Her nipples stiffened in the soapy water.

"No," Aja retorted. Steel's big, strong hands massaged her tits, weighing them. "They've swollen," he observed. "Pregnancy suits you."

Aja tried to squirm away from him. She was still a little piqued- he knew she was jealous, but did nothing to assuage her concerns. As usual, Steel wanted to make light of everything!
His arms held her fast to his hard body, preventing her escape. Aja could feel his cock stiffening

against her ass. He couldn't win her like this!

But as his ministrations became more insistent, Aja felt herself yielding to him, her body slackening against his. His fingers delved lower to the soft skin of her pussy. His mouth never left her throat. One hand held her firm against him.

"Are you jealous?" he asked her again.

Aja shook her head. He began to fuck one finger into her pussy. "Don't lie," he whispered. "I want you to say it."

"Unhh..I'm jealous," Aja admitted in a whimper. "I-I'm jealous."

"You're so wet," he murmured. "Wet for me."

Suddenly he leaned back, withdrawing his fingers from her, resting his elbows on the edge of the tub. Aja was caught off guard; was he really going to leave her unsatisfied!?
Steel closed his eyes, pretending to be relaxing. He cracked one open to a slit and caught Aja's glare. He tried to fight off a grin, and failed.

Suddenly he launched himself at her, water exploding around them. Aja shrieked; he lifted her up out of the water and carried her to the bed.

"We're soaking wet!" she protested, but he didn't care. He dumped her on the bed, and by the time his big body had followed her, they were both laughing in earnest.

Aja's stomach was still small, the bump no bigger than a soccer ball between them. Steel lay on his side next to her and stroked it with his palm. In the low light from the storm outside, his eyes glowed like crystals of blue flame.

"Don't be jealous," he said finally. "You're the only woman for me. The only woman I need."
He moved over her and brought his lips to hers in a gentle kiss. Aja opened her mouth to receive him, her little tongue darting against his. The kiss deepened passionately. Even with the water droplets drying on her skin, Aja felt hot, hotter than fire. Steel's

kisses grew more insistent, and he dropped his head lower to suckle gently at her breasts. They stiffened in his mouth like little buds, and he brought them up gently with his teeth, lapped at them softly with his tongue. His fingers worked her all the while, delving inside her softly parting thighs to find the sweet cream slicking against her walls. He made her wetter with his hands and then with his tongue. He plied her depths, sucking at her clit until the storm inside her burst in a shower of stars and fire. Aja arched her back, her hands pushing his curly gold head downward, begging him wordlessly to continue.

This time, he wouldn't stop.

As if sensing his unspoken command, Aja got to her knees on the bed, ass sticking in the air. She took his length into her mouth. Her head bobbed on his cock; she needed no direction. Steel had taught her how he liked her to suck him off, and Aja was an apt student. Spit coated and bubbled over his dick. He slid into her mouth to the back of her throat, until she had taken him to the hilt. His balls slapping her chin with every stroke, Steel leaned back on his elbows to watch his black queen work for his orgasm. She stroked his cock with her mouth. It twitched and jumped inside her velvelty oral walls. Her tongue lapped at the sensitive head, and her mouth came down over the shaft so he was really and truly plowing into her throat.

Aja's wet and warm mouth was all the heaven he needed. "Good girl," Steel groaned. She took his velvety balls in her mouth next, her brown eyes flicking up at him, wide and sensuous. Aja could feel the veins in his dick swelling as he mouth-fucked her, his balls tightening up against the shaft as Steel readied to blow his load down her throat..

With all the strength he had, Steel held back from cumming down Aja's pretty throat and coating her face with his seed. Though she was pregnant already, he still liked pumping her full of cum. He would fuck her senseless every day that he could, as he had already been doing.

"Lie on your back," he whispered, authority in his voice. Aja complied willingly. She would always do as he said when they were in bed; she liked when he took command of her. She liked how he could bring her to unbelievable of heights of pleasure with a word, by taking control of her body and riding her into places she'd never even dreamed of.

He dropped his mouth to her pussy again, lapping at the sweet and salty cream dripping from her pussy. Steel's mouth made love to her for a while, but he still craved a greater release that only her inner wetness could give him.

Steel rubbed his cock in her juices. He coated the head of his shaft; he liked to be slick when he first slid into her, so he could go all the way and hear the little moan escape her lips. Aja's pussy was tight and wet, clamping around his dick like a vise. It took a few strokes to open her up completely, but then once he did it was sweet and felt amazing. Ever since she'd gotten pregnant her pussy felt eleven degrees hotter. It made him want to cum in an instant, but Steel liked taking his time. Aja had her own needs- and he was happy to fulfill them.

He began to slide into her pussy. His cock throbbed heavily inside her. Aja moaned and arched her back, angling him deeper and deeper. His cock, coated with her saliva and her pussy juices, made an easy entry. He held her at the base of his dick, driving it deep inside her so she could feel the full weight and girth of him. He stretched her pussy to accommodate his massive tool. No other man could satisfy her after Steel had claimed her, and Aja wanted no other man but Steel. He levered his hips, pumping into her steamy wetness slowly. Sometimes he did it this way: with forceful, rhythmic thrusts that reached her cervix and drove her into fits.

"Steel," Aja gasped as he increased his pace, hitting her most sensitive spots. A torrent of pleasure flooded her loins. He rode her well, her pussy gripping on his cock as if she were trying to milk it again. Maybe she was. She wanted him to spatter her insides with his seed, or maybe shoot it on her ass- and then finally swallow it all. When Steel held her like this, when he had her cumming on his dick, Aja's mind turned to water and her breasts and pussy went up in flames of ecstasy. She was his woman, and he was her man. They fit together perfectly, locked in a dance of passion older than themselves; older than time.

Bucking over her, Steel withdrew his tumescent love muscle and watched Aja squirm and beg for release. She wanted him to fill her again. She wanted him to keep fucking her as he had. Steel smiled at his beautiful wife and told her to get on her knees. This was his favorite position; Aja knew.

"You're the only one for me," he told her. "Only your pussy. You're mine. I don't give a fuck about anyone else, babe."

"I know," Aja moaned. She knew she'd been wrong to doubt him. Every time he rose her to orgasm he laid claim to her whole body. He was her Steel, he was her fire and thunder. She wanted no one else. No one else could satisfy her like he did.

"Spread it open for me, baby," he murmured. Aja's manicured hands grasped both of her ass cheeks and spread them apart. Her dripping pussy and tiny chocolate asshole were like two treasures. Steel buried his face in her ass, running his tongue up and down the length of it. Her asshole was

tiny and puckered with her
arousal; Steel sucked on it
greedily, returning to her aching
pussy when she began to shake.

He slapped her ass. "Arch your
back. I want to see you take the
whole thing."

She did as he said, gasping
quietly when he slid his member
back inside her. Steel took a
moment to admire Aja's ass,
which, with the pregnancy weight,
was bigger and juicier than ever.
Aja was such a beautiful thick
woman; he loved every hill and
curve of her body, but he
especially loved her ass. He
fucked her slowly, one hand
clamping on the jiggling flesh of
her backside, the other twisting
gently in her hair. He drove her

body down the length of his cock, fucking into her with aching precision.

"Can I touch myself?" she begged.

"Yes baby," he murmured. "Cum on my dick. Make a mess."

"Steel, uhnn...come inside me." "Not yet, sweet," he whispered, his hand wrapping around her throat with agonizing gentleness. He pulled her up, still impaled on his cock, so her soft throat was against his lips. Then he bit her hard. She shrieked in surprise, but the next moment he had covered the spot with a feathery kiss. This was how they played at love together, hot fire and freezing ice, with pleasure and with pain. Once, Steel had bent Aja over his knee and spanked her until she was wet and sobbing, begging for more. Her ass had been sore for two days, but the orgasm he gave her with his fingers, his tongue and then his cock had left her glowing for a week. He liked keeping her primed and ready for him, and Aja liked when he rose suddenly to claim her.

Her ass rode his cock expertly- the other reason that Steel liked this position was that he could watch the frothy cream slathering over his dick. Aja's pussy was wet and steamy, and hot, hotter than he could believe. It was perfect for taking his cum, and he intended to deposit two loads in her before he was finished.

The first one was boiling up from his balls already, and this time he let it shoot inside Aja's willing and needy passage. She cried out in orgasm, shaking all along the length of his cock, but Steel held her fast there and drove into her, forcing his sizeable load deeper into her body, where it belonged. Aja was crying and calling his name, overtaken by the maelstrom of pleasure that ripped through her. But when she turned over, her eyes wet and dark with need, Steel knew that she still wasn't finished. She wanted more, and so did he. He watched her fingers slide down to her sopping pussy.

"Greedy girl," he muttered approvingly. He moved up over her so she could clean his cock off while she touched herself. Her tongue slid over his length, slurping at their combined juices. Steel liked to keep his woman well fed.

"Keep touching your pussy," he instructed, and began stroking his own heavy cock over her. Aja looked up at Steel Gray, her husband, her lover. Every inch of him was roped in muscle. He'd lost weight since coming to Texas, but it only made him harder, more packed with muscle. Leaning over her with his hair a cloud of burnished gold, his eyes flashing like two blue chips of ice, he looked like a Greek god. He could have been carved in marble by a sculptor's hand. The tool he stroked between his legs brought Aja pleasure like nothing else in the world. It was responsible for the life growing inside her womb right now, and she expected to ripen with his seed again and again in the future. They would live in comfort for the rest of their lives, and he would breed her fertile womb as long as they saw fit. Aja felt herself dampen with desire even more, the cum on her fingers working as lube for her needy clit. She stroked herself to orgasm as Steel watched, his gaze triumphant and loving. Squirming and mewling under him, her enormous dusky breasts splayed over her chest, she was the vision of beauty and womanhood. He groped one of her massive tits, feeling its weight with his hands. Christ. He wanted to take her again.

Steel groaned as he slid back into her. The tip of his dick was still sensitive. But he would move for her again. He stroked her slowly, thrusting. Her pussy cradled him. It drew his body down over hers. He leaned his weight on his forearms. The rhythm he kept had Aja gasping in shock and pleasure. He increased his speed, driving into her with abandon. Aja couldn't think straight. Nothing kept her afloat but the furious thrusts of Steel's cock, and finally it broke over her like a tsunami, driving all thought and reason and function from her mind.

***

They lay in bed together afterward, the sounds of the storm breaking over their heads. Steel grinned; Aja was asleep already. She looked like a goddess when she slept, her hair unbrushed and tangled, one hand resting on her face. Her eyes were closed. The impossibly long lashes- one of the first things he'd noticed when they met- brushed against her cheeks. Her cherubic face was so still and peaceful. But Steel knew that it hid an inner strength. An aggression, a drive that no one could stamp out. No matter what Aja had been through, she always managed to bounce back. She was a strong black woman, but she had her weaknesses too, and Steel Gray loved both her strength and her fragility.

He thought about everything that had happened in the past year. At Grandpa Buck's funeral, Aja had been very composed. It was harder on the boys- no matter what, they had loved poor old Buck fiercely, and it was hard to reconcile how he had gone out. His death had been terrible, but as Aja had confided in Steel later, she'd known such an extraordinary man couldn't have had an ordinary death. They gave him an extravagant funeral, the likes of which had never been seen in Boyd. People from all over flocked to attend. Some came all the way from Washitaw. Black folks and white folks; even a few Cherokee. And Buck was interred with his beloved Sara, and their daughter Mamie, at last. Aja commissioned a sculpture to be erected over the site. It was engraved with the following quote:

For the Lord takes delight in his people; he crowns the humble with salvation. - Psalm 149:4.

Then they had sold the Robinson land. Carson had been angry about the destruction of the Tucker House, but he admitted that the fires hadn't been their fault. He was much angrier when the Will came out, to find that two thirds of his inheritance now belonged to the same family he'd told his cousin to avoid at all costs.

Yet Fiona Tucker's Will was clear, and her wishes were fulfilled. Aja found herself the heir to a sizeable fortune, and Steel felt it was time to bring his own inheritance up to her. They had laughed and held each other, content that the rest of their lives would be lived in modest comfort. All three of Aja's brothers- well, her brothers and Drew, her son- could go to college with no expenses spared, with enough left over for any children she and Steel might have.

Aja came clean to Drew

Boyd became a distant memory. In time, the only thing Aja liked to remember about it was her beloved grandfather and mother, and the ageless blue mountains that kept watch over them all.

Dear Reader,

Please visit Jamila Jasper's website to win three free e-books as well as a free audiobook, unavailable anywhere else.

www.jamilajasperromance.com

Thank you very much for reading this story; I hope you enjoyed it.

Best,

Jamila

Made in the USA
Coppell, TX
14 August 2020

33088172R00288